FINDING
HOME

A Willow Bay novel

by Laurie Ryan

www.laurieryanauthor.com

Dedication

To my brothers, who might not like being a dedication in a romance novel, but they are the heroes I design my life by. And they are all about family, which is a huge part of this story.

Chapter One

Gladys pushed a grocery cart piled high with who-knew-what along the sidewalk. People driving by must have wondered how the frail-looking woman managed it, but there was steel beneath that feigned fragility. The persona had served her well so far.

"Almost to the pizza joint," she mumbled. "Halfway home."

Thankfully, the May weather was moderate and patches of sunshine graced the beaches. The street Gladys walked was long, one of two main roads in the ocean-side town of Willow Bay. Traffic had picked up, which meant more tourists. Good. Willow Bay needed tourists. Barely past a long, hard winter, most of the businesses could use the pick-me-up.

For her, the day was just about over. She had almost reached the red sign of Square Peg Pizza Parlor that marked her halfway-home point. All had seemed well in Willow Bay as she'd walked her route checking on the town. It was time for her to rest. She wasn't as young as she used to be.

A rustling in the bushes next to the building got her attention.

"Who's there?"

The leaves stopped moving, so she pushed her cart beyond the pizza parlor door, out of sight of the bushes. She then rounded the building and pounced, coming up with a ragamuffin teen who wore more dirt than clothes, if Gladys's eyes—and nose—were still any good.

"What are you doing in the bushes, girl?"

Startling blue eyes glared back at her as the girl remained mute.

"Well, if you won't tell me, maybe you'll tell the owner of this establishment. Come on." She grabbed her by the ear and walked her to the front of the building and inside. It was early, so there were no customers in the dining area.

She tugged the girl, who continued to glare at her, toward a chair. "Sit." Leaning over the counter, she hollered toward the kitchen. "Bernie!"

~~~

"Gladys?" Bernie came out wiping her hands on a towel. She smiled when she saw the white-haired woman wrapped in her usual layers of clothing. "I was wondering if I'd see you today. Want some pizza?"

"Nah. You gave me enough yesterday to feed me for a week. Thank you very much for that." Gladys patted Bernie's cheek. "I brought you a stray."

Bernie leaned sideways to see behind Gladys. "A stray?"

"Yeah. You collect them, don't you? Find them homes?"

"Stray animals, Gladys. Animals. Who's this?"

"I don't know. Found her rustling around outside your place. Didn't look like she was up to much good."

Bernie edged around the counter to stand in front of the girl. Young, maybe preteen by the look. Hard to tell through all that familiar dirt. Bernie sniffed. Been a while since the kid had bathed, too. She leaned in for a closer look and the girl yanked her head back.

"Don't touch me."

Warning bells jangled in Bernie's head. She knew this defensive posture too well. Damn.

"What do you want to do with her?" Gladys asked, having sat in a nearby chair.

Bernie watched the girl for a long moment, then took a deep breath and let it out slowly, shuddering at memories she still couldn't quell at the age of thirty-two. She should call Social Services and let them deal with the kid. That was the right thing to do. At least, that's what the law said. She knew differently. The idea of sending those angry blue eyes off to some foster home didn't sit well. Some were good. Some? Well, not so much. Bernie rubbed her churning stomach. She couldn't believe she was about to do this. "Leave her with me, Gladys. I have an idea or two."

"Whooeee." Gladys turned to the girl. "You're in trouble now. This one,"—she pointed at Bernie—"doesn't take shit off anyone."

Laughing, the old lady shuffled outside. Both Bernie and the girl watched her shove her tarp-covered cart back onto the sidewalk and get on her way.

"Old bag," the girl muttered.

Bernie took a step closer, hands on hips. "I ever hear you badmouth Gladys or anyone in this town, I'll call child services to pick you up before you finish the sentence."

All the attitude disappeared as fear entered the girl's wide eyes. Man, she was in a world of hurt. They both were, because it looked like Bernie had taken this little problem on. She should just call child services and be done with her.

Except Bernie knew that system personally, and it destroyed kids. It wasn't meant to. It should protect them, but it was what it was.

"You hungry?"

The fear receded and a quick hit of hope filled the teen's

face before she covered it up with street swagger. "Could eat."

"Yeah. Thought so. You were rummaging in the garbage for food, right?" She didn't wait for an answer, turning to head back behind the counter. "Follow me."

In the kitchen, Bernie pointed to a door. "Wash up. I'll make you a pizza. Pepperoni?"

The girl opened her mouth, then closed it again. Finally, the war within her subsided enough for her to mumble, "cheese."

"Got it. Go clean up as best you can. You can use one of the towels in there. Fifteen minutes to pizza."

The girl disappeared inside the small bathroom and Bernie slumped against the counter. What had she gotten herself into? Obviously frightened and alone, the kid looked like she hadn't eaten in days. *Damn it. Damn it. Damn it.* That kind of gnawing hunger would drive a person to do just about anything.

Shaking her head, she made a large cheese pizza and shoved it in the oven.

When the girl came out a few minutes later, her face and hands were noticeably cleaner and her hair was hidden under a bandana. She kept her head down and sat where Bernie indicated, staring at the glass of milk in front of her.

"Yes, that's for you. There's more if you need it."

"Th-thank you," the girl muttered.

She drained the glass and Bernie refilled it as a bell went off.

"That's your pizza. I'll be right back."

Bernie purposely left the girl alone, wondering if she'd run or stay for food. That she'd thanked Bernie said a lot. The kid knew how to appreciate help when she got it, but it didn't look like much help had come her way in a while. Bernie attacked the hot pizza with the cutter.

Gratified that the girl had stayed, Bernie didn't immediately set the pizza down, letting the smell of melted cheese and sauce help her gather some information. "Tit for tat," she said. "I need a name."

The girl stiffened.

"Just a first name. I have to call you something."

When she finally spoke, it was like each syllable had to be dragged out of her mouth. "I-Irene."

That was a bald-faced lie. But it was something. Bernie set the pizza down in front of *Irene* and sat across the table from her.

Irene didn't immediately dive in. She actually placed a napkin on her lap, settled her small plate front and center, then dished up a slice, covering it in parmesan cheese.

Girl likes cheese. Bernie hid a smile. "Not sure where you got Irene from, but with your permission, I'll call you Ren."

The quick jerk of the kid's head didn't go unnoticed. Ren must be close to her real name.

After she'd eaten two slices, Bernie asked the next question. "How old are you?"

That defiant chin came up again. "Old enough to take care of myself."

Yes, and she was doing such a good job of it.

"How old?"

"Sixteen."

"Bullshit. Twelve."

"I don't look twelve and you know it."

"Right around there."

There was that little chin-jerk again. Twelve was close, so thirteen or fourteen was probably accurate.

Bernie's cell phone rang. She wrote down a takeout order as she watched the kid eat. Four pieces, then she stopped. Probably hoping to save the rest for later. On the street, food was always half now, half for the starving times. Damn, but this kid didn't deserve this. No kid did. Bernie hung her head for a moment, wondering how she was going to handle this with everything else she had going on. She couldn't put the kid out on the street. She thought about how the girl shied away from any touch. Bernie wasn't ready to turn her in until she knew more about her story.

Decision made, Bernie stood and grabbed a box. "Box the pizza and come with me."

They walked outside and up the stairs on the side of the building.

"Aren't you going to lock the doors?" Ren asked.

"No need. This is a safe town." Bernie stopped at the door and looked at the girl. "Unless you have an accomplice?"

Ren shook her head.

"Good."

Inside Bernie's small two-bedroom, one-bath apartment, Bernie took the pizza and put it in the fridge. "This is the main living space, as you can see." She tried to perceive it through Ren's eyes. In contrast to the dark wood of the pizza parlor below, Bernie had painted the paneling in pastel ocean colors. The furniture was old but comfortable. To her, it was an oasis. To Ren, it had to be heaven.

She walked down the hall, assuming the girl would follow. She did.

"Laundry room," she said, pointing to one side. "You know how to use a washer and dryer?"

Ren nodded.

"Good. I have to go back downstairs and work. You are welcome to wash your clothes." She pushed the next door open, showing the bathroom. "And you can shower and use whatever you need. Blue towels are yours."

Ren's eyes got wider.

"This closed door is my bedroom. Stay out. And don't think I won't know if you go in there, even if only to look around. Trust me, I'll know."

Opening the last door, she walked inside the small guest room. There were boxes piled up on the full-sized bed, stuff Bernie just never got around to sorting.

"You can sleep here. Pile the boxes in front of the closet for now."

"Y-you'll let me stay?"

"Trial run. For tonight." Bernie stayed by the door so the kid didn't feel threatened, but lowered her voice to the timbre that reined in the Thompson's twins when they were tearing around her restaurant. "You betray me, you do something to lose my trust, and you're out. You got that?"

Ren nodded her head so hard Bernie almost laughed.

"All right then. Make yourself comfortable. I close at nine."

She walked out the door and downstairs to get that take-out order going, wondering the whole time what kind of huge mistake she'd just made.

Chapter Two

Paul Gibson stepped out of his car and took a deep breath. In all his forty years, he'd never grown tired of the ocean. Something about places like Willow Bay called to him, so he'd snatched up the opportunity to be here. His job usually meant visiting less desirable neighborhoods and this was a nice change. The salty air invigorated him, though he'd never done more than visit the beach once or twice a year. Work kept him too busy.

He frowned. The case that had brought him here was complicated, but the tip had been credible, so he'd been authorized to check it out for a few days with the understanding that the less days away from the office, the better.

Reaching into his gray sedan, he pulled out a laptop bag and a gym bag, then headed inside the hotel-turned-rental condos where he'd reserved a room for the week. The Beachwind wasn't the most expensive place in town but he'd booked the top floor, unwilling to squander the chance for a view. He let himself into a room that smelled a bit musty but made him smile with all the beach paraphernalia. Everything looked clean and neat. He set his bags down on the slightly threadbare couch and walked straight to the sliding glass door. He opened it and stepped outside.

Dunes kept ocean weather from eroding the town's land, so the water was a ways off. Still, he could see the waves cresting and hear the subtle roar of the sea as it rushed to steal what it could from the beach.

What a view. Paul would never get tired of it. He took another long, cleansing breath and felt the tension of the city, the job, and life falling away. He could live in a place like this.

Even the temperature felt good, a nice warm May day.

Back inside the condo, he left the slider open to air the place out, then unpacked and set up his laptop. By now it was close to dinner time, so he shot his boss a quick email to say he'd arrived and decided to find a place for some food and a beer. He reached into his laptop bag for a picture of his missing person and tucked it into his pocket. He headed out to his car but quickly decided against driving. Better to walk, something he generally only did in a gym these days. The beach called, but his stomach grumbled, so he listened to its complaint and walked toward town. A block over, he was back on the main road in and out of Willow Bay. There were more hotels, a Thai place, and a pizza joint.

Choosing pizza, he headed that way. Inside, he took a moment to appreciate all the antiques scattered through the room and the wooden carvings peppered in amongst the tables. The walls were covered with posters, license plates, and various farm implements, and lanterns hung from the ceiling. He could spend a day just checking it all out. And the pizza smells! When was the last time he'd indulged himself in a sit-down, leisurely dinner? He ate on the run or packed sandwiches. Nothing fancy. Food was food. At least, it was until he'd walked in here.

"Have a seat anywhere. I'll be with you in a moment." The mass of burnished copper curls belonging to the voice whizzed past him with a pizza perched on one hand. If the smell was any indication—and in his case, it was—this had been the right choice. Pepperoni, pizza sauce, and the yeasty dough smells made his mouth water. There were a few seats at the counter, so Paul settled into one of them.

"What can I get you?" Curls said, walking past him and around the end of the bar. He got his first good look at the waitress and almost reached up to push his jaw back into place. Those rich curls framed a heart-shaped face with the perfect dotting of freckles and the greenest eyes he'd ever seen. She was tall, too. Probably just shy of six feet and, while she'd never be described as petite, she had curves in all the right places. He'd always liked petite women, but he might have to rethink that.

"Sir?"

With a mental shake, Paul got back in the game. "Sorry. I got distracted." *By you.* "What did you ask?"

Her smile was friendly and wide, and it drew him right in. Into her. He damn near leaned forward.

"What'll you have?"

Food. Drink. Dinner. That's what he came for. "A beer. Bottle if you have it. I'm not picky on brand. And the pizza smells great."

"Tastes just as good," she said, leaning down to open a bottom cupboard fridge and pull out a beer.

God, even her ass was perfect. Paul resituated himself against a tightening he hadn't felt in a long time.

"Beer," she said, setting it in front of him. "Now, what kind of pizza can I make you?"

"You're the cook?"

"Worse. I own the joint."

"Nice place."

She glanced around, nodding. "I like it. So... do you want to tell me what kind of pizza you want, or should I surprise you?"

Chuckling, Paul glanced up at the menu board, tempted to go with his usual sausage and pepperoni until he saw the manager's special.

"What's the special tonight?"

"It's a rich meat pizza with my own little twist."

"Then that's what I'll have."

"Okay, so surprise it is."

"Bernie?" The family two tables over called out.

"Be right there." She tapped a hand in front of Paul. "Be about twenty minutes on the pizza. Just holler out if you need another beer. Two's the limit here, though. Just so you know."

"Will do." Paul watched her wander through the restaurant, checking on customers. There were two men in a booth toward the back. When she laughed at something they said, the sound mesmerized him. Her laugh was all in. He suspected her attitude toward life was the same.

He wiped dew drops off his cold beer, remembering when he used to be like that. His job had sucked the life out of him. For sixteen years, he'd been trying to do what was best. He could never please everyone. Someone was always angry or afraid, and it was overwhelming. He'd spent more and more time lately wondering about a change. Maybe it was time to find something completely different, something that fed his soul. He liked helping the kids and had thought it was his calling, but lately, no one was happy no matter what he did. And then there was Georgie.

Don't go there. Paul shook his head, driving the boy's face deep into his subconscious mind. It wasn't easy to forget your worst mistake. Because of that case, Paul now towed the regulation line. No more letting the situation dictate the choices. There were rules and he was damn well going to follow them.

When his pizza was set in front of him, Paul took a sniff. "This smells like heaven."

"It's my own recipe." She touched the edge of the platter. "You'll have to let me know if you like it."

"I will."

She went to take the family's payment and Paul dished up a slice, reaching for the parmesan and red peppers, then thinking twice about it. He wanted to try this pizza on its own merit. One bite in, he knew he'd made the right choice.

"How is it?" Bernie asked as she passed with her arms full of dirty dishes.

Unwilling to stop chewing, Paul gave her a thumbs up-sign, and her face lit with a smile. He dug in with a vengeance and forgot everything for a while. Somehow, another beer appeared in front of him. Paul kept eating, closing his eyes often to savor the taste. Four pieces later, he pushed the pizza back and looked around, surprised to see the place had emptied.

"Want a box?"

"I could keep going, but yes, I'll take a box."

She pulled one out from under the counter and slid his pizza into it.

"That is just about the best pizza I've ever eaten."

"Thank you. We aim to please."

"Do you use the same dough for all your pizzas?"

"I make the dough myself and use the same dough recipe, but for this pizza, it's herb-infused."

"The combination of meats and sauce and dough was great. I don't recognize the cheese."

"That's because I make that myself, too. Only use it on this pizza."

"You should enter a contest or something. This is that good."

Bernie reached behind her to tap the blue ribbon hanging on the cash register. "Already have."

Paul held out his hand. "I'm Paul Gibson. You're... Bernie, I think I overheard?"

"Yep." Bernie shook his hand, hers calloused, his smooth. Paul wanted to hold onto that hand for as long as possible, but she quickly pulled back.

"You're not local."

"No. I'm from Vancouver. Washington, not B.C."

"Around here, we're close enough, so that's the

assumption."

"Yes, but I get asked that question so much, I qualify it without thinking."

Bernie chuckled. Once again, he admired the throaty elegance of her laughter.

"Are you here for an early vacation? The weather's been nicer than usual for May, so you picked a good time."

"A working vacation." Paul dug the picture out of his pocket. "I'm looking for this girl."

If he hadn't been looking right at Bernie when he turned the picture around, he'd never have noticed the slight tightening. She hid her reaction well. Most people would have missed it, but Paul's job depended on reading body language. Bernie had just tensed up and he had no idea why.

She leaned forward for a better look. "I don't think I've seen her." Straightening, she stepped back. "Why are you looking for her?"

Paul pulled a card out of his wallet and laid it on the counter. "I work for Child Protective Services."

This time, almost anyone would have noticed Bernie stiffen. There was something about CPS that she didn't like.

He pointed to the picture again. "She's an at-risk runaway."

"Endangered how?"

"She's only thirteen. Living on the streets... well, she'll be both vulnerable and gullible. I'm sure you've heard stories."

That head nod was pretty stilted. What was going on with her?

"What was her home life like?"

"I'm not sure. Still sussing that out. I thought things were stable for her, but this is the second time she's run, so I wanted to follow up this lead right away."

"Lead?"

"Yes. We got an anonymous call." He glanced at his watch. "Gosh, only about three hours ago. The person said the girl might be hanging out around here."

"Well, good luck." Why did it sound like she was pulling her teeth to spit the words out? Something must be going on.

"Since I don't have any more customers, I'm going to close early if you don't mind," Bernie said.

"Not at all." Paul smiled, trying to find their earlier camaraderie. He wanted to get to know Bernie, but her stone-like expression didn't waver. He set some bills on the counter and stood. "Keep the change."

"Thanks." Bernie stayed where she was, hugging the towel she used to clean the counters to her chest.

"Good night," Paul said.

"Good night."

Darkness had descended, along with a chilly wind. Paul tucked his coat in tighter and headed back to his hotel. The entire time, he couldn't get Bernie out of his mind. Beautiful in a roller-derby queen sort of way, she intrigued him. And the fact that she didn't seem to care much for what he did for a living intrigued him.

He glanced back to see the lights turn off. Bernie locked the front door, then headed up the stairs. She must live above the restaurant.

Square Peg Pizza had been put to sleep for the night. Paul turned back toward his hotel, knowing his own sleep would be disturbed with thoughts of the restaurant's owner and wondering about her story.

He would find out. One way or the other. Paul wasn't sure why this was important to him, but now he had two reasons to stick around Willow Bay for a while.

~~~

"Oh shit, oh shit, oh shit," Bernie muttered as she

entered her apartment. "What the hell have you gotten yourself into?" She looked around, expecting to find Ren catching up on teenage television. The T.V. was off. In the kitchen, dishes Bernie hadn't washed were drying in the drainer. She opened the fridge and pulled out a beer, then counted how many were left. None were missing. And was that disinfectant she smelled? Had the kid actually cleaned?

After tip-toeing down the hall, she opened the spare bedroom door, glad she kept them oiled. Ren was in bed, tucked up under the covers fast asleep. Bernie closed the door just as quietly and checked the bathroom. No mess at all. Ren's towel hung over the shower rod drying. And she could tell the washer and dryer had been used because the load of towels she'd never folded now sat neatly on top.

Bernie took a long pull on her beer as she sank into the couch cushions. This kid was an enigma. A runaway, but a neat one. A mostly polite one. What was her story? Burning with curiosity, she wanted to wake the girl up, but she probably hadn't slept well in weeks. They'd have to sort it out tomorrow.

Quietly and away from prying eyes, apparently. How could Ren and the man searching for her have both shown up at Square Peg on the same day? The oversized CPS chip on Bernie's shoulder made it hard for her to believe Paul was a good guy. Up until she'd found out what he did for a living, she'd liked him, with his disheveled, light brown hair and laughing blue eyes. Liked him maybe a bit too much, damn it. Why couldn't he be a carpenter or a doctor? Even a lawyer would be better than CPS.

A flash of memory stole Bernie's breath. Being manhandled into a car and taken back. To him. No one would listen to her. No one even tried to understand. She couldn't go back. She just couldn't. She kicked out, hitting the lady right in the knee. Then she ran, praying the whole way she hadn't seriously hurt the woman.

Bernie shook her head and took another sip of her beer. That had been a long time ago. She'd carved out a nice life for herself. She got along with almost everyone in Willow Bay and even had a best friend in the mayor, Josh Morgan, who'd just found his forever love.

No way Bernie wanted to risk screwing things up for herself. Maybe she should turn the girl in. The thought made her hang her head. She couldn't do that. Not without more information, which meant there was nothing more she could do tonight.

She dumped the rest of the beer and headed for her room. She could lie in bed trying to solve unsolvable issues same as on the couch, but a lot more comfortably.

Chapter Three

Paul walked along the sandy beach that stretched as far as he could see, staring at the ocean, listening to its roar and the gulls calling. The sound was louder here, but not overpowering. He'd have to come back in winter, do some real storm-watching. Everything about the place calmed him, even with his near sleepless night. His weather app said it would be sunny, but he couldn't tell from the cloud layer that merged with ocean and sand. Still, it worked for him.

The beach was so wide, he thought the tide must be out. He needed to pick up a tide table. Paul pulled off his sandals and let his toes sink into the wet sand at the waterline. If he stood still, the sand eroded beneath his feet, a strange sensation. A little further up, he found an intact sand dollar. Poor thing gave its life to the tide, getting washed up. Paul wrapped it in his handkerchief and put it in his pocket, a memento of the rare peace offered by this morning.

Not compelled to walk or do anything, he stood there breathing in the ocean air, watching the waves. A fishing boat slowly motored along the coastline, adding to the serenity of the moment. A lone runner jogged his way, slowing to a walk near him, then stopping, hands on knees as he caught his breath.

"Good morning," he said after a bit, his sandy hair blowing in the ever-present breeze.

"Hi."

"Enjoying the beach?"

"Yes. I used to come here as a kid." Paul looked out at the waves. "I forgot how nice it is here. Peaceful."

The man chuckled. "Not always peaceful, but you picked a great day to be here. I'm Josh, by the way. Josh

Morgan, mayor of this little hamlet."

Paul shook his hand. "Paul Gibson. Nice to meet you. Place doesn't look a whole lot different from when I was a kid."

Josh chuckled. "If you only knew. We've tried to keep the small-town flavor of Willow Bay. This, though, is the biggest draw." He waved his hand at the ocean.

"That it is."

"You here on vacation?"

"Working vacation. Speaking of which... " Paul pulled a business card out and handed it to Josh. Then he showed him the picture. "I'm trying to find this girl. She's an endangered runaway. Her family is looking for her. Have you seen her?"

"I hate to hear of kids living on the streets. That's the biggest crime there is. Damn." He peered closely at the picture and shook his head. "I'm sorry. I haven't seen her." He pulled his phone out of a pocket. "Can I take a picture myself? I'd like to keep an eye out for her, and I can pass this around through email to our agencies."

"Sure." Paul held out the picture. "I'd appreciate that."

Josh fingered the card. "Is your cell phone on here?"

"Yes. I'm all over the place with this job, so that's the best way to get a hold of me."

"Good. Now, I'd better get back. The job is waiting. Nice meeting you, Paul. I hope I'll see you around Willow Bay."

"I'll probably be here a few days, so maybe."

With a wave, Josh started back along his path at a jog. Paul watched him for a minute, then turned to his own workday.

~~~

"We need to talk," Bernie told Ren over breakfast. Bernie never cooked a hot breakfast. Not when she spent all day in a kitchen. They ate cereal at the retro green and metal table Bernie had bought second hand, not caring that it had a couple chips in the laminate on top. It had been too cool to pass up.

Ren looked at her warily. Bernie slid the card she'd been fingering all morning—Paul Gibson's card—across the table and Ren's eyes widened. She stood up, slamming the table in her haste. "I have to go. I've gotta get out of here."

"Hang on," Bernie said, waving her back down to her seat. "You're safe at the moment, so let's figure this out."

Ren didn't sit back down, but she didn't run off, either. Bernie took it as a sign that the kid didn't like being on the run.

"Why are you helping me?"

Bernie kept her gaze steady. "Because I've been where you are."

The indecision was plain on Ren's face. The pull of fight or flight, the law of the land for a runaway. You ran whenever you could, and if that wasn't an option, you stood your ground and fought. Bernie waited, giving Ren time to sort it out in her head.

Finally, after the room grew so quiet Bernie could hear her antique clock ticking, Ren sat back down.

"Good," Bernie said. "You just took the first step toward getting your life back in order."

"I can't stay here," Ren said.

"That's not necessarily true, but before I can figure out how to help, I need to know your story. Will you tell me?"

This was the toughest question to ask a runaway, especially one that had been on the streets for a while. Kids who got pissed at their parents and ran away to make a statement generally didn't last long before crawling back home. The ones who stayed, who preferred the streets over what they had at home, had a rough story to tell. Rarely would they give out that information.

Ren started tearing the edges of her napkin, minuscule piece by minuscule piece. "What do you want to know?"

Bernie opted to start with the easy stuff. "How long have you been on the streets?"

"Two months."

"Okay."

"Two months, six days, eleven hours."

Oh, yeah. Bernie knew that count. It could make you crazy and also keep you sane, figuring out how long you'd been fending for yourself.

"How long were you out there on your own?" Ren asked.

If she wanted Ren to trust her, she had to be willing to give as good as she got. "I never went back. I carved out a life for myself that didn't have anything to do with the alcoholics who were my biological parents."

Ren nodded.

"Is that what happened to you?" Bernie asked quietly.

Ren shredded more napkin, her head down. Her lashes glistened with tears that dropped onto the pile of paper debris. "My mom died."

"Oh, man, that's rough."

"Yeah, but not as rough as the old man she lived with at the time."

"Your father?"

"Hell, no." Ren looked up, defiance clear in her gaze as she swiped at wet cheeks. "My dad was some army guy in town on leave, according to my mom. I never knew him."

Lots of things to deal with here. They could search for her real father if they could find out more information about him. But first things first.

"So, the boyfriend."

"A mean one. Mom died in a fall. I think he did it, but

no one would listen to me. So I decided to not become his next victim." Her chin jutted up a bit further.

"Good self-preservation, kid. So why is CPS looking for you? How are you in their system?"

"Well, this isn't exactly the first time I've run."

A perennial runner? Bernie didn't think so. This was clearly situational.

"I ran away once before. Made it two weeks before they caught me. Apparently, the boyfriend filed a missing person's report."

"Why would he do that?"

Ren shrugged. "Not sure. Except, well, he's a control freak. Maybe he didn't like me not obeying him?"

Could very well be. Bernie had seen that mentality in her mother many times. "So when you got caught— "

"They didn't send me back right away. I went into foster care."

The tiny bedroom with two sets of bunk beds flashed through Bernie's mind. She knew about foster care, too.

"Somehow, though, he convinced them to make him my guardian and they sent me back to that house." Ren took a deep breath. "The first time he hit me, I hit him back with everything I had. Knocked him to the floor, grabbed the backpack I always kept ready, and ran. That was two months ago."

She turned to stare out the window.

Bernie's heart about broke. This kid had been through so much, it wasn't fair. At all.

"I'd better get going," Ren said, standing.

"Not so fast. I'm not sure that's necessary."

"What do you mean?" Ren sank back down on the chair.

"I mean, if you leave, there's a better chance someone will spot you." Bernie tapped the card on the table. "If this social worker is worth his salt, he'll be going around town showing your picture, maybe even pinning it up in the grocery store and other places." With those blue eyes that could laugh just as easily as they could go dark and serious, Paul Gibson was most likely very good at his job. Otherwise, he wouldn't be the one out on the road searching. That took a special kind of devotion.

"Right, so I need to get out of here."

"Or you can hide." Bernie couldn't quite explain it, but she didn't want Ren to go. No one had helped her when she'd been desperate. She didn't want this kid to have the same problem. With what little time they'd had together, she'd seen a quiet, polite, organized kid underneath the streetwise veneer. Ren deserved a shot at a decent life and Bernie wanted to give her a leg up. Plus, if she stayed, it would give Bernie some time to dig into her bio-dad, see if they could find him.

"Here?"

Bernie shrugged. "Why not? It's better than the streets."

"I think I'd feel trapped."

"I get that. You can help out in the restaurant if we can get you down the stairs with no one seeing. But beyond that, you're right. Until this guy is gone, you'd pretty much be stuck in this apartment."

Ren got up, walked to the window, and looked outside. Fight or flight. What would she do? After a couple minutes, she turned back to Bernie. "I guess we could try it."

Bernie wanted to fist-pump air but settled for tapping her leg with happy fists beneath the table.

"For a couple days," Ren said. "If things get dicey, though, I'm gone."

Bernie smiled. There was her street-smart kid. "Okay. For a couple days. Then we'll reevaluate."

"What about that old biddie, I mean, uh, old lady who found me?"

"I'll talk to Gladys. She'll keep quiet."

"Then I guess we have a plan."

"We do. With one caveat. You do some online work while you're here. School type stuff."

Ren shook her head, but couldn't quite hide the flash of excitement in her eyes.

"That's my requirement," Bernie said.

"I guess... I guess I could give it a try."

"Great. We'll set that up tonight. In the meantime, let's go downstairs and get ready for the day."

Ren headed for her room, but Bernie sat at the table a while longer. Picking up the business card, she stared at it, flicking the edge with her thumb. Last night, in a rare moment of clarity, she'd wanted to get to know Paul Gibson, an urge that hadn't surfaced since Tristan. Her life back then had been a bitter battle between her heart and her will to live.

Once again, she was stuck between two very immovable rocks. What was best for Ren had to be the priority at the moment.

Maybe one of these days, it would finally be her turn. She could follow the whim of her attraction, stare into dreamy blue eyes, laugh at jokes only they understood. Maybe share her life, both the good and the bad. Bernie rubbed at the tightness in her chest. Thinking about what-ifs never helped. Pushing the chair back, she stood, tossed the card in the basket of oranges on the table, and went to get ready for what she could control. Her day, the restaurant, helping Ren. That's what had to matter. Nothing else.

Later, while working in the kitchen with Ren, Bernie kept glancing at the empty bar stool. She's always been able to compartmentalize. File unwanted emotions away until she had a safe place to deal with them.

So why wasn't that working now?

Chapter Four

Bernie ate her salad as she waited for the evening to pick up, customer-wise, though more time was spent following the striations in the wood countertop with her finger than eating. Today had been a day of revelations. She'd had plenty of time to think them all through, yet not a single solution had presented itself.

First and foremost, Ren was a hard worker. She'd set her to inventorying supplies and an hour later had gotten a neat list. She'd even highlighted items that she thought were getting low. The kid was a thinker. Then, together, they'd made dough for the day. God, Bernie loved that yeasty scent. It bothered some people, but apparently not Ren, who'd thrown herself into mixing and kneading. They were completely different when it came to measuring out ingredients. Bernie threw in the amount that looked right. Ren filled the measuring cup, tapped it, ran a knife across the top, and inspected it before emptying it in the mixer.

When customers came in during the lunch hour, Ren stayed in the back, out of sight. She read the orders as Bernie brought them back and grabbed ingredients while Bernie made the pizzas.

The restaurant would soon be full and there wasn't much more to do besides make pizzas as ordered, so Ren went back upstairs with a lasagna they'd made together. It had been a good day. A surprising one. Bernie, always a loner, had enjoyed the kid's company. And that spelled trouble with a capital "T." Plus, that damn social worker kept invading her thoughts. Bernie didn't get hooked on people. She had friends, and Willow Bay's mayor was as close as she'd come to caring for someone. Okay, Dana, his fiance', too. But life had taught Bernie to rely on herself and no one else. She didn't want to like Ren, but it was too late. The kid wasn't meant to be on the streets. She had potential, and too much good in her.

The door jangled. "Hey, Bernie," Josh said. Dana, his fiancé, waved.

Seeing her good friend and his fiancé always made Bernie smile. It had taken Josh so long to let Dana know he was interested. They'd been inseparable since their mutual declaration of love. They'd found each other. Sometimes, Bernie wondered if she'd ever find someone she could trust so totally.

"Hi," she said, giving herself a mental shake. "How's it going?"

"Good," Dana said. "Business is picking up at the gift shop now that the weather's getting nice."

"Which means she's much happier these days," Josh said. Dana smacked him in the shoulder.

"It's getting busier here, too. The same locals and more tourists."

"Good news all around. Are you coming to the planning meeting this weekend for the Beer and Chowder Festival?"

Bernie looked at the ceiling for a moment. "I want to. If business allows."

"Awesome. Dana and I have been working on our own version of seafood chowder for the contest."

"Now that we have a working kitchen," Dana said.

Bernie had seen the before and after versions of the mansion Josh had been renovating. He had upped the timeline and gotten some help thanks to Dana's "I'm not moving in until there's a working kitchen" ultimatum.

"You did a great job with the renovations," she told Josh, who grinned.

"Got any lasagna?"

"Only for my favorite people. The usual pizza for you, Dana?"

"No, I think I'll share the lasagna."

"Wow, that's a switch."

Dana laughed. "What can I say? I'm a convert. Everything you make is amazing."

Bernie headed for the kitchen and packaged up a lasagna for them. Josh handed over his credit card. "Oh, by the way," he said, digging out his phone. "I met a guy this morning. He's looking for a girl, a runaway."

It took every bit of strength Bernie had to not stiffen. She focused on running Josh's card, hoping no one noticed how tightly she held onto the card reader. "Oh?"

"Yes. Here's a picture." Bernie glanced at his phone. There was Ren, younger, happier. The same picture Paul had shown her last night.

"Have you seen anyone like her?"

Not willing to lie to her best friends, Bernie hedged. "What would a kid like that do around someone like me?"

It was Josh's turn to laugh. "You are a bit rough around the edges when it comes to kids."

"It's not that I don't like them. I just never spent much time around them." Bernie handed the sack with the lasagna to Josh. "Bake at 350 degrees for half an hour and it should get nice and bubbly for you."

Josh leaned over the register to peck Bernie on the cheek. Dana smiled and waved goodbye.

"See you later," they said in unison.

Bernie clutched the counter as she watched them climb into Josh's SUV. The noose was tightening. If Josh knew about Ren, then the CPS guy was working his way through town. That couldn't be good.

Farther down the street, Bernie saw Gladys pushing her cart along. She had no idea where Gladys spent her nights.

She'd asked her, as had Josh and Dana and half the people in town, but she wasn't forthcoming. The woman wouldn't take help from any of them, except maybe some food. All Bernie could do was hope she had a place to sleep out of the rain.

Walking around the counter, Bernie stepped outdoors and waved. "Hi, Gladys. Need any food to get you through tonight?"

"Ah, thanks, dearie, but I'm fine. Got enough leftovers right here." She patted her cart.

"Okay, well, let me know if you do. Oh, hey, you know that girl you brought in yesterday?"

"The one trying to steal from you?"

"She wasn't stealing. She was hungry. Anyhow, ummm, there's a guy in town looking for her."

Gladys's stare drilled right through Bernie to the real issue. "And you don't want him to find her."

"It's complicated. He's with CPS, but... well, I'm not sure that's the best thing for her."

"I knew she would be in good hands with you." Gladys patted Bernie's hand. "And your secret is safe with me." She made a locking motion over her lips, then pushed on to who knows where. Bernie watched her walk off. Gladys was an enigma. She didn't want much help, didn't want to stay in the local shelter, yet always seemed to be around when Willow Bay needed a hand, like some sort of homeless fairy godmother.

"Good evening."

Bernie jumped at the voice, whirling around. Paul Gibson stood a few feet from her.

Crap. Had he heard their discussion? His smile seemed natural, his stance relaxed. The jeans he wore fit snugly and the Henley shirt looked well-filled out. Unusual for a man who worked at a desk. Damn, but he looked good. That tightness resurfaced in Bernie's chest and she fought the urge to rub it.

"Hi," she said. "Back for dinner?"

"I've got leftovers from last night, but thought I'd pop in for one of those beers."

"Sure." She led the way back inside and headed behind the counter to safety. If her walk was a bit fast, she blamed it on the evening chill starting to settle on Willow Bay.

"Same thing as last night?"

"That would be perfect."

She grabbed one, popped the cap, and set it in front of him, praying to God that Ren didn't decide to come downstairs. They'd talked about the importance of her staying out of sight for the time being, but you just never knew with teenagers. Maybe the wifi bugged out or the fridge quit working.

"A bit slow, eh?"

"Mid-week tends to be slow. It'll pick up." Bernie leaned back against the beer cooler. "Any luck finding that girl?"

Paul frowned. "No. Not one bite."

"I'm sorry." The white lie didn't come off her lips easily. Bernie preferred no answer at all to a lie. This was no way to start a relationship.

She froze. Relationship? Where the hell had that come from? *Shit.* She shoved the thought—kicking and screaming—into one of those compartments in her brain.

"I'm sorry, too," Paul said. "She's so young, and just lost her mother. She's so vulnerable right now. The wrong guy..."

Yeah, Bernie knew about that. Thankfully, she'd steered clear. Mostly.

Paul took a swig of his beer. "Yep. As good as it tasted last night."

"Thanks. It's my version of an amber IPA." She leaned

over for a whiff of the pungent beer, one of the best she'd ever concocted.

"You made this?"

Bernie laughed. "You sound surprised. Yes, I make beer. Even though my parents were alcoholics."

He cocked an eyebrow. "That's highly unusual."

"It's my way of telling heredity to shove it. And it reminds me that I am not my parents. But they're the reason I have a two-drink limit here."

Paul nodded, taking another sip. "They still around? Your parents, I mean."

"Nope. Both dead." Now, why had Bernie told him any of that? Hell, only Josh knew anything about her past and he didn't know much. She never spoke of her parents to anyone, so why had she opened up to this relative stranger? She'd need to be wary around him. Apparently, he had a way of drawing out information. Maybe it was the calm, peaceful inflection of his low-timbred voice. Or the light in his eyes as he focused on her, making her feel like the only person in the world at that moment. Time to change the subject.

"Sad, that the kid you're looking for lost her mother. Is her father looking for her, then?"

"Her legal guardian, the mother's boyfriend. He seems concerned about making sure she's safe at home with him."

"Seems?"

"Yeah. The guy is perfect on paper."

"I sense a 'but.'"

Paul nodded. "I can't put my finger on what I don't like. But I know that, when I find Ren, I'm not sending her back home this time until I answer that question for myself." He stared off into the distance, a haunted look aging his face for a moment until he shook it off.

Just when Bernie wanted to distrust this man, he went all vulnerable and tugged at her heartstrings. She couldn't stand anything, animal or human, being lost or alone. "That's an unusual position for a CPS worker to take."

"It's not standard operating procedure, but it's not outside the rulebook. To be honest, we have very little power when it comes to things like delaying the return of runaway children to a bad home. If we don't have proof of any issues, we have to send them back."

Paul fixated on his beer, deep in thought. Was there something in his past? Had something gone wrong? She wanted to reach over, touch him, bring the smile back to his face. Instead, she hugged herself and waited, letting him think.

When he shook his head, she almost jumped, they'd been so quiet for so long.

"Sounds like you have some experience with CPS," Paul said.

That hit too close to home. "A little."

"Care to share?"

Bernie shook her head. "I don't know you well enough."

"All right. How about we rectify that?"

"What do you mean?"

"Have dinner with me. You get a night off once in a while, right?"

She laughed to cover her nervousness. "No. Not really."

"Come on. All work and no play?"

"Keeps a restaurant open and operating in the green. Mostly." She turned to wipe down the soda station. If he were any other man... Paul's rugged handsomeness didn't match his office job. His sharp blue eyes, that disheveled hair that gave him a "just got out of bed" look, tugged at her. For the first time in a long time, she wanted to spend time with a guy, get to know him better. To see if he just might be the one to break the celibacy she'd held herself in for so long.

Except, he couldn't be the guy. He was looking for the

stoic, ultra-organized girl who currently sat upstairs trying to figure out her life. Until Bernie had a better idea of what was best for Ren, she couldn't go near Paul Gibson. Not with a ten-foot pole. No siree.

Paul took a sip of his beer, watching her. "When do you open?"

Operating hours were clearly listed on the door. "Two p.m."

"Breakfast, then. Or hell, just coffee. I probably have to head home tomorrow unless I get a hit on this girl's whereabouts. I'd like to visit with you for a while before I go."

Bernie leaned against the back counter. "Why?"

"Because you interest me, and no one has done that for a long time. I'd like to get to know you better." With his direct gaze, the honesty in his words was hard to deny. But why her? He said it himself: all work and no play. Her life was dull.

"You're only here for one more day?"

"Unless I get a lead. But Vancouver isn't that far. Look, I'm not asking you to marry me."

He paused as if surprised he'd said that. Bernie was glad of it. She needed a moment to hide her shock.

"Just... coffee," he said. "Let's take some time to get to know each other and decide if this is something we should pursue."

The way his eyes darkened, that last word almost made Bernie shiver. God, it had been so long. "All right," she whispered. This was such a bad idea.

"Woohoo!" Paul slapped his hands on the counter.

Bernie chuckled.

Just then the door opened.

"Hi, Connie, Charlie." The couple that walked in ran the café across from Dana's gift shop. It must be date night, an evening away from their kids, something they'd started when Charlie finally got back to construction work after the long winter. "Take a seat anywhere and I'll be right with you."

They picked a booth near the front. Bernie reached for her order pad, then rounded the counter close to Paul. Too close. He reached for her free hand, tugging her attention toward him. His hand was warm and comfortable. Bernie liked the feeling.

"I'm glad you agreed to coffee. See you at the café in the morning?"

At Connie's? Where just about everyone in town had breakfast? "Ummm, no. How about the coffee place just as you come into town?" She pulled her hand from his and stuck it in her pocket.

"Keeping us secret from the town, eh?"

The man knew how to read her too well. "There is no us."

"Not yet." Paul plunked a couple bills on the counter, stood, and pecked her on the cheek. "See you tomorrow. 10 a.m."

Bernie touched the lingering warmth where he'd kissed her. Out of the corner of her eye, she saw Connie's graying pixie-cut as the woman leaned out of the booth to stare at her. *Damn.* All she needed was for the town to think she was dating someone. Bernie had managed to stay under the radar for a long time and didn't like being the center of attention.

She looked up at the ceiling, where she hadn't heard even one footfall. Meeting Paul was bad on so many levels. But she'd agreed, so she'd show up. And nip anything he thought they might have in the bud. Men weren't part of her life. They only complicated things. So better to meet him in broad daylight and make a clean break.

Resolute about the plan in her mind and refusing once again to rub that unfamiliar ache in her chest, Bernie headed over to take orders. Now, if she could just get her heart to catch up with her brain.

~~~

The next morning, Paul sat in the aromatic little coffee shop, half expecting Bernie to no-show. She'd looked like a scared rabbit last night and the fixer in him wanted to understand why. She was a beautiful woman. Not petite, but not overly muscled, either. Curves in all the right places, and those Irish green eyes lit a fire in him every time he saw her. He wanted to thread his fingers through those copper curls of hers. Kiss lips that had haunted him since he'd met her. But more than that. There was a mystery behind her and he wanted to know it. Understand it. Solve it.

He looked around. Not much traffic here this time of the morning mid-week. Only two people had come in since he'd sat down. He'd shown the girl's picture to the barista, who'd shaken her head. An anonymous phone call had brought him to this town. Was it a wild goose chase? With no other sightings, he'd have to head back to Vancouver today.

Damn. He'd only met with the teenager once and her wide, fearful, blue eyes had gotten to him. Paul looked out the window. All the kids tugged at his heart, especially the ones he couldn't help. But this one... She'd told him her mother had been killed, but with every official report indicating it was accidental, he'd had to tell her the police couldn't pursue it. After that, the girl had clammed up. She hadn't said another word as he'd tried to help her. He'd had no choice but to send her back to her legal guardian, though something nagged at him about the man. He'd planned to keep close track of them but never got the chance. The girl had disappeared within twenty-four hours of being sent home.

That had been weeks ago. This was the first clue he'd

gotten to her whereabouts. He really wanted to find out why she didn't want to live with her guardian. If she had a good enough reason, this time he'd try to make things happen for her. As much as he could. His hands were tied, now more than ever before, thanks to rules, regulations, and a few kids who'd sadly slipped through the cracks. Paul understood the need for rules, but they frustrated him sometimes and kept him from doing what would help the children the most—finding a happy place for them to thrive. A place where they'd be loved. Cared for. That was all he wanted.

Not that he got that result often enough.

Paul spied Bernie walking up to the door and shook off his morose thoughts. Just seeing her made him smile and lightened his heart. He stood.

"Hey," she said as she joined him, stiff posture and all.

"Good morning. I'm glad you came."

"Did you think I'd no-show?"

"I'll admit the thought crossed my mind."

"Well, something you'll learn about me is that I do what I say I will."

"Duly learned. Do you want some coffee?"

Bernie, still looking endearingly like a deer in headlights, nodded her head and they both ordered coffees. Settled back against the high-backed chairs at their table, she looked out the window. Paul took a minute to gaze at her. The curls had been tamed back into a clip, mostly. Her cheeks were flushed, and, when she turned back to him, he could see she was tired.

"Seems like you're working pretty hard. Has it always been that way?" he asked.

"Running your own business means long hours, but working hard gives me a good life, so I don't mind." She looked at him. "What about your job? A nine to five?"

"Hardly." It was Paul's turn to gaze out the window.

"Seems like it could be a tough job, being part of the system. If you're trying to help kids, that is."

Her statement told Paul a lot. Only people who'd been in "the system" called it that. Plus, she knew some didn't care and just put in their hours, though thankfully they were few and far between. Paul would bet a year's salary that she'd been in the system herself, and hadn't gotten the help she needed.

"Pretty much all of the people I work with care and try hard. We work long hours searching for kids and solutions."

"Not everyone does that." Bernie looked down, toying with her coffee cup.

Paul leaned over and tipped her chin up, saw the miserable memories written on her face. "You were a foster kid."

"And a runaway." She held her head higher.

"Because of your parents?"

Bernie shook her head. "I don't know you well enough to have that conversation."

Damn, but she was locked down tight. "All right. I can understand that. So, what do you do for fun around here?"

She chuckled at the change of subject. "Long hours at work, remember? I don't have time for fun. But I do like to hit the beach, especially at low tide, to see what's floated in. And I like to listen to the ocean. You have to like that to live here because it's a constant process to keep buildings and cars and things from deteriorating due to the sea air."

"I think it's worth it. I went for a walk on the beach yesterday. I couldn't believe how good it felt."

"You don't live that far. You should visit more."

"Like you said, long hours. Though,"—he reached for one of her hands— "I might have to amend that."

Her eyes widened as she stared at their hands.

Paul ran his thumb along her skin, surprised at how soft

it was. With all that pizza-making and washing, he'd expected rough, work-worn hands. She had callouses, but otherwise, her skin was smooth and unblemished.

"I'd like to get to know you better, Bernie."

"Isn't that what we're doing right now?"

"I'd like to go on dates, take you for walks on the beach, see where you live."

Bernie stiffened and pulled her hand away, which confused Paul. He felt the connection between them every time their eyes met. So why was she unwilling to see where it would go?

"I'm sorry." Bernie stood up. "This was a mistake. I need to go." She looked at him. "I really am very sorry."

She damn near ran out of the coffee shop, leaving Paul surprised and confused. What just happened? All he'd said was that he wanted to get to know her better. Her eyes, such a vivid green, had been wide, almost tearing up. Full of sadness, but there'd been something else. Something Paul only saw in the faces of children who didn't want to go back home.

Panic.

Chapter Five

Bernie drove the two miles home in a fog after her conversation with Paul, having to slow her speed twice. All she needed was for Jackson, Willow Bay's sheriff, to pull her over in her current state. She swiped at her face, trying to quell tears she hadn't cried... ever.

I think there's something between us.

She'd never felt an inkling of emotion for any man until Paul showed up. The man, after so short a time, had become an itch she couldn't scratch. The fact that she wanted to scratch it so badly scared her worse than anything. Better off on her own, she'd guarded her heart all these years. So why was this happening now? Why Paul Gibson? She would not, could not get involved with him. For Ren's sake. Really, that was the reason. Besides, she'd lied to him. He'd walk into her apartment and see Ren and it would all be over anyhow, so there was no sense even trying.

The thought of it being over before it even began filled Bernie with melancholy. Somehow, Paul Gibson, child counselor, had gotten under her skin.

She slapped the steering wheel and slowed her speed. Again. *Damn it.* No one got through her defenses. Absolutely no one. Not since Tristan. She'd learned that lesson the hard way.

Besides, right now, it was all about stabilizing Ren's life. She couldn't think about hers until she sorted Ren's out. That had to be her focus.

Bernie pulled into her parking spot. She had time before the restaurant opened, so she headed upstairs. Once inside, she smiled, letting the coziness calm her. Ren sat at the computer desk drinking coffee, doing homework on a site

Bernie had found for her.

"This place is cleaner than it's ever been."

Ren shrugged. "Figured I'd better do something to earn my keep."

"Well, it's appreciated. How's the school stuff going?"

"It's mostly review so far."

"Want to bump up a grade?"

"No. The review is good. Gets me back in practice."

Bernie poured a cup of coffee to replace the full one she'd left on the table at the coffee shop.

"Let's talk for a minute," she said, sitting on the couch.

"'Kay," Ren said, twirling around in the office chair to face Bernie, her worried face ramping up to the defiant, block-it-all-out kid she'd been two days ago. Had it only been two days?

"I'd like to try and find your biological father but I don't want to do anything behind your back. How would you feel about that?"

Ren chewed on her lip as she twirled in the chair. One circle, then another.

"I'm not sure," she finally said. "I've always wondered about him, but what if it put me in a worse situation? And what if he didn't want me at all?" This last was almost a whisper.

Ah, damn. This kid deserved love and reminders of how special she was, not the beating she'd gotten so far in life. Bernie saw the chink in her armor. A sheen of tears the kid refused to shed. To be unwanted was the penultimate worry of runaways. Well, right after surviving and not getting physically hurt. Most needed out of the situation they were in, but they also wanted to find a place to fit in. Their place. To know they were worthy and not the trash they'd been convinced they were.

"It's a risk. But if you don't want to go back to your

mother's boyfriend, I think it's your best bet."

"I kind of hoped I could stay here with you."

Bernie didn't know how she felt about that. Ren was quickly, quietly winding her way around Bernie's heart, but to take on a kid when she barely made it on her own?

"I like you, kid."

Ren's face fell. The "show no emotion" wall crashed down, shuttering her expression.

"Don't go all street on me. Let me finish. I like you. And maybe you staying here would work, but we need to solve your situation first."

The façade slipped away and Ren crumbled in her chair.

"I'm not saying we're going to out you right now. But we need to clear this up, make you a legal kid again."

"The only way to do that is to go back to him."

Ren started to shake. Bernie pulled her out of the chair and into her arms. "I won't let you go back to him. I promise you that." The burden of that promise weighed down her heart. Bernie wasn't one to make promises easily. This one could turn into a life-altering thing, and not necessarily in a good way. She'd fought her way off the streets and didn't relish the idea of going back on the run. Still, a part of her knew, if it came to that, she'd grab Ren and go. Some things were more important than a comfortable life.

Together, they sat on the couch, Ren letting the tears finally fall and Bernie overwhelmed by the promise she'd just made.

"Do you know anything about your dad?"

"Not much." Ren sighed. "He wasn't around long. I'm not sure Mom even told him she was pregnant. She wouldn't ever confirm that, but it's what I've always believed. After all, who walks away from a kid?"

Lots of people, sadly.

"Was your mother... stable? Did she have any mental

health issues?"

"My mom was great," Ren said, stiffening.

"I'm not trying to point fingers, kid. I'm just trying to understand the situation." Okay, back to the dad. Safer territory. "Do you know your dad's name?"

Ren gulped and stood. She *did* know his name. Bernie would bet anything on it. But divulging it meant giving too much of herself away. Bernie understood that fear. She'd lived with it for too many years, finally dealing with her past once she'd figured out she wanted a future. No one could figure it out for someone else, so she would wait. She'd let Ren decide in her own time.

"I haven't trusted anyone since my mother passed away."

"I know. If you need some time, that's okay. We can manage for a while like this. But not too long, okay? I don't like the subterfuge." Or keeping secrets from Paul Gibson. When he'd laid it all out on the line this morning, she'd panicked, which wasn't something Bernie Pedersen ever did. She dealt with situations through honesty and blunt forthrightness. Yet this morning, she'd been a scared mess and had run rather than deal. Well, at least she wouldn't have a CPS guy hanging around while she and Ren figured things out. Paul Gibson was probably already on his way back to Vancouver.

Rubbing the unusual ache in her heart, Bernie stood. "We'd better get things set up for the day downstairs. Want to help?"

"You bet." Ren jumped up, clearly eager for anything that wasn't a discussion about her past. They headed downstairs to make dough and trimmings. Bernie kept a close eye out for anyone who fit the tall and handsome category. For Ren's sake. At least, that's what she told herself.

~~~

Paul checked out of his condo and stuffed his duffle and computer case in the trunk, slamming it a little harder than necessary. Nothing about leaving felt right. He hadn't gotten a single lead on the girl since that one anonymous phone call. Had this been nothing but a wild goose chase?

An impression of green eyes reminded him that something good had happened here. He'd met Bernie. Beautiful, strong, street-smart Bernie, who'd run at the mention of a date. Who peered at him from behind walls he wasn't sure could ever be pulled down. Paul knew those kinds of walls. He'd erected plenty of his own, mostly due to his job. If you couldn't compartmentalize the emotion, you didn't last long as a CPS social worker.

Bernie, though, had taken those barricades to a whole new level. And Paul, more tired than he'd been in a long time, wasn't sure he had the strength or patience to wear her down enough to give him a chance.

He drove out of town, slowing as he passed Square Peg Pizza. No sign of activity yet. Too early. He reached the highway and sped up, away from Willow Bay, back to the life he'd settled into after college. A life that no longer held anything he loved, if it ever had. When he'd graduated from the University of Washington with his master's in social work, he'd been ready to fight the world to make life better for the children who would lead it someday. Now, he was just tired. He couldn't effect change and rarely felt he was helping the kids under his supervision. So why was he doing this? Why was he chasing down runaways just to send them back to the same situation?

Everything seemed so futile these days. Paul spent the two-hour drive back to his apartment trying to figure out how to be more content in his life. With every turn of a corner, the answer flashed in front of him like a neon light—

curvy, curly-locked, and staring at him with forthright green eyes.

Bernie.

He missed seeing her already, and he barely knew her. How did she get under his skin so fast, especially when she had her own version of armadillo hide keeping him at bay?

Inside his apartment, he unpacked, put on some mellow music, and opened the fridge to find it empty except for beer. Reaching for his phone, he ordered a burger meal, then grabbed a beer, not caring that it was early afternoon. It was five o'clock somewhere, right?

He took a long pull, then grimaced at the taste. This sure wasn't as good as that Square Peg IPA. And just like that, he'd gone back to thinking about her. *Damn it.*

Unable to think his way out of the mood he'd settled into, Paul poured the beer out and headed for a shower. Maybe he could wash the last couple days out of his system.

Not likely.

Chapter Six

At 9:30 that night, Bernie locked the restaurant doors and headed upstairs, more deflated than she'd been in a while. Something had gotten a hold of her, an unfamiliar melancholy, and she didn't like it. She knew right where it came from, too. Thoughts of the long-gone social worker kept invading her day.

The apartment was dark except for a light over the stove. Ren had left a note saying she was in her room with her earbuds in.

Bernie sank onto the couch. She had no energy to shower and go to bed. Everything weighed on her. Ren, keeping Square Peg in the green, everything. But mostly, she regretted not giving Paul Gibson a chance. She'd wanted to, though it scared her more than anything. How could someone captivate her so quickly?

Not that it mattered. He'd left town. That damn chest ache started in again and Bernie refused to give in and rub it. Better to close it off, let it go. There were more important things to worry about than Paul Gibson, right?

Her phone rang. She glanced at the clock. 10:15? No one called her this time of night. She didn't recognize the number, either, so she didn't answer. After a bit, the phone pinged indicating she had a message, so she hit speaker.

"Hey," the deep voice said.

Bernie's breath hitched and she sat up straighter.

"It's Paul. I assumed the restaurant number was also your personal number. If it's not, you'll get this tomorrow, I guess. I just—Well, we didn't leave things very well this morning and I wanted to know you were all right. This is my cell, so call anytime. Anytime. Really. Okay, I'm hanging up now. Hope to talk to you soon."

The voice faded and Bernie clutched her phone tight. He'd called. An unusual emotion filled her. Relief. Happiness. Giddy, crazy, barely-able-to-contain-herself happiness.

She added him to her contact list, then sat there staring at her phone. Should she call him back or wait? What was socially acceptable these days? Who cared? He'd called her. For once, Bernie didn't think about complications or how messed up this could get. She hit the button to call, giving in, just this once, to what she wanted to do more than anything in the world.

"Bernie?"

"Yes." God, why did she sound so breathless? "I didn't recognize your number when you called. I don't generally answer calls I don't know after hours."

"Good for you. So I was right that this is your cell?"

"Yes."

"Good."

A silence hung between them, as if neither knew where to go from here.

"I'm sorry I ran out this morning," Bernie said.

"I was worried about you," Paul said, at the same time. They both chuckled.

"I guess," Bernie said, "this morning surprised me."

"That's been a constant for me since I first drove into Willow Bay."

"There's nothing much interesting in our little town. Or about me, for that matter."

Fishing for compliments? Where had that come from? Bernie had given up asking for validation from others a long, long time ago, so what was it about this guy that made her seek it now? The silence expanded between them and a warning voice echoed in her head. Bernie steeled herself for the letdown, the tone of his voice that would tell her everything. He'd called because that's the kind of guy he was, but she wasn't his type.

"I think," Paul said quietly, "you underestimate yourself."

Yep. There it was. *Wait, what?* Bernie held her breath, listening to the voice in her head rewind and play the words again. An unfamiliar warmth filled her at the understated, yet very powerful compliment. Bernie fiddled with the edge fringe of a couch pillow.

"Bernie? You still there?"

"Yes. Just… digesting your compliment."

"Well, thank you for not calling it flattery, because it wasn't. You tug at me."

"Ditto. You're a hard man to forget."

"Good." His voice held a softness, a gentility she hadn't heard before. Is this how he sounded late at night? She clutched the pillow tight, wishing she could settle inside warm, comfortable arms. Another foreign concept, but one she'd figure out later.

Besides, Paul wasn't in Willow Bay anymore.

And she had a runaway in the next room.

Bernie sat up. She cleared her throat, digging for the bravado that had helped her squelch unwanted emotions so many times before, trying not to think about the fact that, now, she wanted these feelings.

"So you're back in Vancouver?"

"Yes, and missing your pizza and beer, among other things."

"What's life like for you there?"

"Work, gym, takeout, sleep. That's pretty much it."

"Sounds familiar, without the gym. Beach walks and carrying trays full of food and drink. That's my workout."

"I think I like yours better than mine."

She laughed until she heard Ren step across the hall, a reminder of what was at stake. God, she really shouldn't be doing this. Why did she have to meet someone interesting now, of all times?

"I'd like to try again," Paul said.

"Try what again?" The bathroom light came on and the door closed.

"You. Us. Dating."

Dating. Wouldn't that be nice. Being carefree, laughing, not thinking about all the problems of daily life. Enjoying someone's company with the possibility of... Nope. Not going there. Celibacy. That was her lot in life, at least until she figured out a few things.

The bathroom door opened. Ren shut off the light and went back into her bedroom.

Yep. Celibacy.

"You don't talk much, do you?" Paul said.

"I like to think before I speak."

"Nothing wrong with that. So about that dating thing?"

"We live hours away from each other, Paul."

"Only two. I'm happy to drive your way. Or we could meet somewhere."

"I don't know. My life is... complicated right now."

Paul didn't answer for a moment. "Complicated how?"

"I'm not at liberty to discuss it. I just... I need some time."

"All right. I can understand that. I'm disappointed, but I understand. So, is there too much going on for the occasional phone call from a new, uh, friend?"

Bernie smiled and relaxed into the couch pillows again. This guy was the quintessential mediator and compromiser. She liked that about him. "No. I think I could manage that."

"Then we have a plan. But now, it's late and we both have work tomorrow, eh? Sleep well, Bernie."

Her name rolled off his lips like an ocean swell, moving slowly, mesmerizing.

"You too. Goodnight."

She disconnected and sat there staring at her phone, warmth seeping past all the immovable shields that surrounded her heart. Not so immovable after all. Somehow, Paul Gibson had wormed his way into her life in a single day. Bernie set the pillow aside and got up, unsure how she felt about this upheaval. Somehow, she'd gone from the daily grind she knew and trusted to one fraught with innuendo and worry. She headed down the hall to her bedroom. She noticed the light go off under Ren's door and knew that this girl was the more important issue.

Still, a part of her wished that, just for once, she could let go, enjoy life, and forget everything that had come before. To think of a future.

~~~

Paul walked out on his patio and looked at the dark woods that bordered his condo complex. The night chill soothed him, as did the darkness. But the call to Bernie? That had both settled him and worried him. What was going on in her life that she thought dating him was too much to add to the mix? She was about as closed off as a person could get. Maybe it came from what street life had been like for her, or maybe something situational, going on now. Hell, a combination of the two could be deadly to any relationship.

Paul liked fixing things, making them better. He wanted to help Bernie, but until she opened up to him, that wasn't possible. Still, she'd called him back. And she'd agreed to the occasional phone call. Paul smiled, knowing he'd be hard-pressed to wait more than twenty-four hours to hear that hearty laugh of hers and listen to that guarded-but-comforting voice again. Getting her to lower those tightly-built defenses wouldn't be easy.

He headed for bed, knowing he wanted to do exactly that. All he needed was a plan and a lot of patience. A whole lot.

Chapter Seven

Late April rain had given way to a tentative sunshine and Bernie took advantage of it, heading for the beach and a barefoot walk in the sand. She wanted to bring Ren, but until they resolved her situation, it wasn't a good idea. Over the weekend, they'd talked more, but Ren still held back on the hard facts. The girl couldn't stay with Bernie much longer without someone finding out. Without a bio-dad name or something they could use to move forward, Ren's life was on hold. And so was Bernie's.

Well, mostly on hold. Water lapped at her ankles, carrying a cracked shell past her as the tide rolled in. Life rolled like that, an ebb and flow. Right now, she was in an ebb, with one exception. Bernie smiled. Paul had called three nights in a row. Last night, she'd surprised him by calling just before his usual time.

"This is a nice surprise," he'd said.

"Repaying the favor," she'd said, heaving a long sigh of contentment at the happiness in his voice.

"Talking to you is the highlight of my day."

Hers, too. "I'm getting used to finishing out my day like this."

"One of these days, we'll have to try it in person."

The thought of him, here with her, or her with him, had seemed so right. She could picture it, see herself wrapped in his arms on the couch. Bernie Pedersen, who'd never needed anyone to help her settle, found herself wanting that more and more with each passing day. Soon. Hopefully soon.

"One of these days."

"How about this weekend?"

Reality had crashed in, popping the contentment

balloon she'd climbed inside. "Maybe not this weekend. But soon."

Bernie kicked at a piece of seaweed. Paul had gone quiet after that, clearly surprised. The call had ended shortly after that, without the usual calm. Bernie didn't like stringing him along, but she obviously couldn't explain her situation. At least, not yet.

With a glance at her watch, Bernie headed away from the water and back into town. She waved to Luke Taylor, the town's resident Mr. Fix It, who had a fishing line strung out into the water. She dried her feet, slipped on her flips, and headed for the grocery store. Normally, she got restaurant supplies from a wholesaler in Aberdeen, but Ren had noticed she was nearly out of the ingredients for her special sauce.

"Hey, Sam," she said as she emptied her fuller than expected cart onto the conveyor.

Sam, a behemoth of a guy with a full head of white hair and startling blue eyes, was Willow Bay's most prominent confirmed bachelor. Several of the senior women shopped for groceries daily in hopes of catching his interest, but he'd held tight to his status. At sixty, and with that twinkle in his eye, he should be dating. But if he was, Bernie didn't know who or how. He was always at the store when she came by. Having opened it with his wife who'd passed away several years ago, it might well be that tie that kept him from moving on.

"Hi, Bernadette."

She shook her head. "You know I hate that name."

"But I love it, and you should be used to it by now."

"Yeah, yeah, yeah."

He scanned items, holding up the bag of garlic. "Making your special sauce again?"

"Shhh. No one's supposed to know what's in it."

He zipped his lip. "Not my rumor to spread."

Bernie laughed and, after bagging her groceries, headed out to her car. As she shut the hatchback, she heard the familiar jangle of grocery cart wheels and turned to see Gladys heading her way.

"Just the lady I was hoping to see," Gladys said, leaning in. "How's our girl doing?"

"Just fine," Bernie said. "My apartment is cleaner than it's ever been, if you can believe it."

"Good. I like it when someone who needs help deserves help. Any luck with her situation?"

"We're working on it, but it's slow going. Hard to trust anyone when your faith has been shattered."

Gladys peered at Bernie, pursing her lips. "I'd imagine you'd know more about that than most."

Bewildered about how Gladys could know anything about her personal situation, Bernie hesitated. Gladys, never one to let time get away from her, tucked things into her cart. "Well, I'd better get along. Day's not getting any younger and neither am I."

"Want a ride?" Bernie already knew the answer to the question, asked and answered so many times.

"I'll make it just fine on my own. Not far to my digs from here."

Gladys clapped a hand over her mouth at the same time Bernie's eyes widened at this piece of information slipped from Willow Bay's best secret-keeper.

"You stay around here?" Bernie glanced around, trying to figure out where a homeless person could find shelter from the weather. Mostly a commercial area, with the grocery, law office, gym, and Josh's CPA office, there were no houses or motels. And not much vegetation to get beneath.

"I don't stay anywhere," Gladys said, her composure quickly back in place. "I'm everywhere, and nowhere."

Apparently, that's all Bernie was going to get in the way of further information. Still, a slip from Gladys was unheard of. Bernie would have to keep a sharp eye out when in the area.

Pushing her cart a couple feet, Gladys stopped and turned back around. "Where's that nice man been? The one that made you blush to high heaven when he walked up to you last week."

Paul? She'd seen Paul? Gladys's home camp now completely forgotten, Bernie hemmed and hawed. "He had to go back home."

"Shame." Gladys cocked her head. "I kind of liked the look of you two together. Well, tata for now."

Bernie put a hand to her cheek. Yep, warm. She never blushed, ever. Yet one mention of Paul and—she checked the rearview mirror as she got behind the wheel—yep, red as a beet. *Damn.* Deciding she'd stop at the hardware store another day, Bernie headed home, her thoughts turning once again to Paul. He'd been disappointed when she'd held him off about this weekend. Bernie, unused to half-truths, wanted to set that record straight. Soon.

Hopefully, very soon.

~~~

Files never stopped finding their way to Paul's desk. It didn't matter that they were digital. He could see the list on his docket, waiting for action. Even working all weekend and all day yesterday, he hadn't made much of a dent. He couldn't ask the other three social workers for help. They were as loaded up with cases as he was.

Still, he'd gotten the most important ones through the system, and had made several home visits to at-risk situations, where he'd found the kids doing well. That helped his sense of well-being, right up until he thought about Bernie. Maybe he should drive back to Willow Bay and talk to her. He could tell she wanted to spend time with him, just as he did with her, but something held her back. He couldn't figure out what.

"You got a minute?" Georgia shifted some papers off the chair next to his desk, plopped them down on said desk, then sat down, her thin frame folding up like an accordion as she settled. At a little over six feet tall, with that white hair and dark skin, she could look most of these parents straight in the eyes and figure out their measure. She might be skinny as a stick, but no one messed with Georgia. He liked that about her.

"Have a seat," Paul said, grinning. Georgia did what she wanted when she wanted, but she was the best darn co-worker he'd ever had the privilege of working with. They all cared, but she went the extra mile.

"How's your caseload going?"

He glanced at the computer. "About as well as yours."

She chuckled, a deep sound that rumbled up from her stomach. "Yes, about as well, I'd guess. You didn't have any luck in that ocean town? Finding the girl?"

"With only the one phone call and no townspeople who said they'd seen her, there wasn't much I could do."

"It's tough when the leads peter out."

"I'm at a loss. Something didn't feel right about her situation. I'd like to get another chance at it, but until I find her, it's a moot point."

"Well, then I'm going to make your day." Georgia reached for the office phone on his desk, put it on speaker, and punched in the password to access their secure, anonymous tip line.

"That lost girl in Willow Bay," a feminine voice said. "The one who was here last week? I saw her again. She's still here, and I think she might be in danger."

That was the entire message. Paul punched in the code

to listen again. Short and sweet and not even any background noise.

"Sounds like the same voice."

"I thought so, too."

"What the hell is going on?" He sank back in his chair. "I feel like I'm on a chessboard and someone's moving my pieces without telling me."

"I get that, but if she's endangered— "

"I don't have a choice but to follow up."

Something at the edge of Paul's awareness wouldn't settle into a solid idea. He was missing something, and he'd better figure it out. Quick.

"So, you going back to Willow Bay?"

"Looks like."

"Good. You came back from there happy. Go find it again." Georgia, thirty years Paul's senior, stood and patted him on the head. "And good luck."

"Thanks." He would need it. Two anonymous phone calls from the same person in a small town where he'd found zero clues as to this kid's whereabouts was beyond strange. Was someone playing him?

He pulled up the teen's picture and stared at it. The last time he'd seen her, she'd been defiant, angry that he'd taken her back to her court-appointed advocate, the deceased mother's boyfriend. She'd run again that same night and Paul hadn't seen her since.

Now she was supposedly in Willow Bay but no one had seen her. Someone had to be keeping secrets.

At least going back to Willow Bay meant he could see Bernie, maybe figure out why she was holding back.

Paul straightened, a notion he didn't want to think about buzzing through his brain. It couldn't be. It just couldn't.

He grabbed his cell phone, told Georgia he'd be back in a day or two, and within half an hour, had packed a bag and gotten on the road.

One way or the other, tonight, he would get some answers.

Chapter Eight

Three hours later, Paul stood across from Square Peg Pizza watching Bernie and the girl come down the stairs, not quite sure what to make of his feelings. He'd been worried about how upset she'd been that day at coffee. Worried and afraid of what she wasn't telling him. Now he knew, and it was his turn to get upset. Betrayed and angry. Is that how he felt? For sure. But also... hurt. *Damn.* He'd barely spent any time with Bernie and already she could hurt his feelings? What a sap he was. Emotional responses like that were exactly the reason he was close to burned out in his job. He cared too much and took it all personally.

The cool air chilled his skin because he hadn't thought to grab a coat. Hell, he hadn't been thinking at all, focused only on finding out the truth. He'd thought Bernie might be the one to distract him. He'd thought... Paul shook his head as he leaned against the side of the building. It didn't matter what he thought. Bernie had lied to him.

"If you lie to me, I'm done with you." Paul told that to every child he tried to help. Bernie wasn't a kid, but she'd broken his number one rule. He rarely gave liars a second chance. Except, he'd stuck to that rule and where had it gotten him? The flash of gunfire, blood, unseeing eyes—the images overwhelmed him. He shook as he tried to shove the memories back into the recesses of his mind.

Paul itched to cross the street and have it out with Bernie. She was endangering this child's life. The girl's family was worried about her. Two steps into the street, he stopped. He was pretty good at taking the measure of a person, a huge part of why he was so good at his job. He'd known Bernie was keeping something from him. She was conflicted, which meant she was doing what she thought was right.

Reluctantly, Paul turned away from the restaurant to find a place to stay. For some reason, Bernie was harboring this girl, and he'd bet anything she had a reason for that. Before he confronted her, he had some digging to do.

Chapter Nine

The next day, Bernie and Ren headed down to the restaurant early in the afternoon to prep for opening. "Cut up the lettuce, okay, kid? About half what you did yesterday. It'll be slower tonight." Bernie marveled at how well Ren had taken to restaurant work. She donned apron, gloves, and hair net without being asked and worked hard at every task Bernie set her. Over the last couple days, Bernie had begun to wonder if she could become a foster parent. Ren needed a home, and they got along well. Bernie sensed a lot of her own personality in the girl, which meant they'd eventually clash some. But that just kept life interesting.

The first order of business was to talk to a lawyer, one who knew family law. Bernie had cleared everything with her own case years ago, including checking in with the social worker she'd kicked to get away. She'd thought she'd hurt her, but it turned out to be a non-issue. The woman hadn't been injured. Still, Bernie's past might keep her from being able to foster Ren.

Bernie squatted in front of the beer fridge to inventory what she'd need from the storeroom and didn't hear the door open. After writing down some numbers, she stood and wheeled right into the chest of the man who'd invaded her thoughts so thoroughly she'd lain awake most nights thinking about him.

"Paul!"

At that same moment, Ren appeared. "Hey, Bernie, we're short on lettuce. Want me to add it to the groc— "

Ren obviously recognized Paul. She whirled and fled, but before she got to the back door, Paul's voice reverberated through the restaurant.

"Stop!" His voice, strong and calm at the same time, got to Bernie.

She froze, automatically following orders. So did Ren.

"Jen, if you run now, you'll be running for a long, long time. I suggest you come back here and"—Paul glared at Bernie—"the two of you explain what the hell is going on."

Her real name was Jen? No wonder the kid had been startled when Bernie decided to call her Ren. It hit too close to home.

"I think he's right, Jen," Bernie said. "You'll be running for a lifetime if you leave now. And your bag is upstairs, so you'll have nothing. I—I don't want you to take off. I'm your friend and I want you to stay."

With her hand still on the door, Jen leaned her forehead against it.

"Please," Bernie said.

Jen turned around, fear and flight stark in her wide eyes.

"I promise," Paul said, holding his hand up like he was taking an oath. "I'll hear you out before taking any action."

The girl's chin came up. "Who else knows I'm here?"

"No one. I only figured it out myself yesterday."

"How?" Bernie asked.

Paul glanced at her. "Too much tension between us, a quick look into your past. A few other things. So I drove back here and saw you two come down the stairs yesterday."

"You arrived yesterday?" The sting of this fact—that he'd been there for a day without telling her—rumbled around her insides like a worm digging for a safe haven. Bernie had always known this secret would kill her chances with Paul, but she'd kept it anyway. Given the choice, she'd do it again because Jen needed her help. Still, it hurt. Right smack dab in a heart that didn't know how to handle Paul Gibson in the first place.

"Yes. I took some time to think things through before

confronting you both."

"Damn," Bernie said.

"Yeah, damn." He turned back to Jen. "Let's talk."

With no small amount of reluctance, Jen let go of the door handle. Bernie breathed a huge sigh of relief. "You promise, right?" she said to Paul. "You'll hear her out before you do anything?"

"I'll hear both of you out," he said, reminding Bernie that she was in just as much trouble as Jen. Maybe more. She'd harbored a minor being sought by the authorities.

"I think we should give him a chance, kid," Bernie said.

Jen walked slowly back in to stand just behind Bernie, who was happy to be her shield.

"All right," Jen said. "But I'm not going back into foster care. And no way am I going back to that man."

"I make no guarantees. There are rules, and you've both broken quite a few of them. But I said I'd listen, and I will. I won't take any action without letting you know what I've decided first. That's the best I can do." He moved to one of the tables and sat down, indicating they should join him.

Bernie felt like a scolded child. The acrid taste of her lies stuck in the back of her throat as she and Jen held hands and joined Paul, taking the chairs across the table from him.

"Let's start at the beginning," Paul suggested.

That lopsided grin of Jen's meant trouble. Bernie already knew that.

"I was born."

Paul rolled his eyes. "Really? How about we fast forward to just before your mother passed away."

"Come on," Bernie said to Jen. "He said he'd listen. This is your chance to get someone official on your side."

"I already tried that with him."

Paul set his hands on the table with slow control and stared at Jen, waiting her out. Good choice, because Jen didn't have as much stubborn in her as Paul did apparently.

"I told you how my mother died." Once Jen decided to talk, she could hardly stop. Even Paul cracked a smile at the plethora of words that fell from her mouth. Over the next quarter-hour, she barely took a breath as she unfolded what life was like in the house of her mother and her mother's boyfriend. She laid out her suspicions about the boyfriend's involvement in her mother's death and the reasons she ran rather than stay there.

"If I'd gone back, I'd be dead by now," she said, tears trickling down her cheeks. "He would have killed me. And no one would listen to me." She glared at Paul. "Including you."

~~~

She was right, damn it all. Paul shook his head. He hadn't listened. She'd told him about the boyfriend and her suspicions and his tired, jaded mind had been convinced she was making it up so she wouldn't have to go back. *Damn, damn, damn.* He needed to take a long vacation after this. He used to be better at ferreting out the real issues. But there had been too many kids, too many parents telling lies.

"You told me before that you don't tolerate lies." New tears fell on Jen's cheeks. "I *never* lied to you. You chose not to believe me."

Man, when a child took you to task and she was right, it really stung. "You're right," Paul said, looking her in the face. "I should have listened better."

He almost laughed at the "ya' think?" expression on both their faces, but this wasn't a laughing matter.

"The first problem, then, is that we need proof of foul play," Paul said. "How do we get that?"

"I don't know." Jen slumped. Bernie put an arm around her shoulders.

"Was there a police investigation into your mother's

death?" Bernie asked.

"The cops, er, police were there, but I don't know if they filed a report or did anything."

"I can check on that," Paul said. "I did a background check on your mother's boyfriend and nothing came up. That's why we let you return to him."

"So there's nothing we can do?" Jen slumped even more. Bernie patted her shoulder.

"I didn't say that. I'll do a deeper dive into him, see if I can come up with anything. But, if that draws a blank, the court order remanding legal guardianship to him might have to stand."

"I'm. Not. Going. Back."

"And I won't let her. I'll file for guardianship to keep her," Bernie said.

Paul could not contain his surprise. From Jen's wide eyes, he judged she was right there with him. She and Bernie hadn't talked about this.

"It's not a rash statement. I've been thinking about it."

"She's been here, what, all of a week or so? And you're ready to take her on full time, permanently?"

Bernie raised her chin. "Jen's a good kid. She deserves a break, and I think I'm the best one to give it to her."

"Don't get your hackles up. In my job, I have to play devil's advocate."

"What about Jen's biological father?" Bernie asked, wariness still filling her eyes.

"What about him? We couldn't find him. Didn't even have a name for him."

"I do," Jen said.

And the secrets keep coming. "You could have told me," Paul said.

"You were the establishment and you didn't listen to me. Why should I have trusted you?"

Paul would bet anything she still didn't. "Well, if you're willing to give me his name, we can try to track him down." He glanced at Bernie. "If we find him, it will affect your attempt at guardianship."

Bernie grabbed Jen's hand and the girl clutched it like a lifeline. "All I know is, this kid isn't going anywhere unless someone proves to me it's a stable situation."

To resolve this, Paul would have to go way out on a shaky limb, he knew. The rules said he should drive Jen back to Vancouver today and turn her over to her guardian. He hadn't listened to her before, and that bothered him. Now he'd heard her out, and honoring his promise meant taking a risk. "Okay. I'm willing to give this a little time. I suggest we make no decisions until we have more information."

He almost laughed as they both exhaled in relief. This wasn't over, though. Not by any standard. "Jen, can you give Bernie and me a few minutes to talk alone?"

Her stink-eye was pretty impressive.

"Don't worry. I won't talk about you."

"All right, but you be nice to her," Jen said, getting up.

"We've got some things to settle."

Bernie turned bright red. Nice to know she recognized the spot she'd put them in.

They listened as Jen clomped upstairs. "Will we hear her if she tries to run?" Paul asked.

"She won't run. She promised to give you a chance." Bernie's laser gaze drilled straight through him. "And you promised advance notice before you do anything."

"Hey, I keep my promises. I'll confess something bugged me from the beginning about her situation. I just couldn't find anything to back it up. But that's not what I want to talk to you about."

"Maybe I'd better get us something to drink."

Paul reached for her, enjoying the feel of hands that had

worked hard but still bore the softness of hope for a better life. "We don't need beer, and the last time we had coffee, you took off on me."

Bernie lifted her hands slightly. "Is that why you're holding on?"

"No. I'm holding on because I like touching you." He did, he realized. All his angst, anger, and sense of betrayal fell away with this simple action. "I like you, Bernie."

Her mouth formed a soft 'o'.

"Like I've told you, I want to get to know you better. Do you still want to get to know me, after all this?"

He watched her closely. Right now, this woman who'd seemed so solid was as skittish as he'd ever seen a person be. She looked as ready to run as Jen did. Speaking of which, Paul cocked an ear toward the ceiling. All quiet. Hopefully, that didn't mean empty.

"Yes. I'd like that," Bernie said, squeezing his hands. "Paul, the only reason I lied to you was to protect Ren. I mean Jen." She shook her head. "Going to take me a while to get used to that name."

"I bet, but you and I have some things to settle before we figure out if there can be anything between us."

Pulling her hands back, Bernie wiped an imaginary spot off the table before she looked at Paul again. "You want to know my story."

"I know the facts. I want the stuff between the lines."

She frowned. "How do you know anything?"

"When I saw Jen with you, I knew I needed some... background. I needed to understand why you were harboring a runaway."

"But you don't even know my last name."

"County deed search." He looked around. "You own this place, so your name is listed."

"But I was underage, and that file was sealed. Besides,

it's all been cleared up."

"Working where I do, I have access to juvenile files."

Bernie's lips became tight lines. Paul could see the conflict in her eyes.

"I know you don't want to rehash the story, but you and I need to get past it. I'm aware that your parents were lifelong alcoholics."

"And you know they're both dead now, too."

Paul nodded. Cirrhosis of the liver. They succumbed to the disease within three months of each other, her father going first.

"You cleared your record right after your mother's death, right?"

She nodded. "I wasn't going to take the chance that they could find me, so I waited. Then, since I was eighteen, I contacted the authorities and resolved the pending assault charges."

"You hit your father with a baseball bat."

"After he beat my mother within an inch of her life." Bernie's chin jutted out.

"And he filed assault charges against you. Why didn't you file against him?"

"No one would listen to me."

Damn. It amazed Paul how much people trusted adults and refused to listen to the kids who were closest to the situation. He sighed. In this instance, he was guilty of the same thing.

"Anyhow," Bernie continued, "the charges were dropped and my record expunged. Or, at least, I thought it was."

"It was." He pulled her hand back into his. "And I'm sorry you had such a rough time of it."

"I came through it all right. I worked hard, saved my money, and bought this place from the retiring owner a few years ago. I'm good."

"Did you keep the name? I've been wondering."

"No. It was Vinnie's Pizza. Didn't think that would work and wasn't thrilled about Bernie's Pizza."

"Square Peg?"

She shrugged. "Square peg, round hole. That's the story of my life. I've never fit anywhere, at least not until I bought this place and made some good friends here in Willow Bay."

"I wish we'd talked about this sooner," Paul said.

"I barely know you and I don't talk about my past with anyone. Not even my friends here."

Paul gestured toward the ceiling. "Does she know?"

"The basics. I didn't go into details."

"Which is why she trusts you. Do you think you could get her biological father's name?"

"If that's what we need to do to fix this for her, I'll get it."

"Okay. And I'm going to dig deeper into the boyfriend. See if Jen's right about him." Paul stood, came around the table, and pulled Bernie up and into his arms. "I want to settle all this and find some time for you and me."

Warmth filled his chest where her hands lay. Paul leaned in and lightly kissed her. "I want to explore everything about us, but I think figuring this out for Jen is more important. Plus, I guarantee you, that girl is upstairs biting her last nail off wondering what we're talking about."

Bernie laughed and laid her head on her hands, against his chest. They stood there for a long moment, rocking back and forth, enjoying each other. Finally, Bernie pulled away. "Dad's name, then restaurant open for the day."

"Text me if you get his name. I'll be in my condo doing research, but I'll come back for dinner."

"Make it late. Say, 8 p.m.? I close early tonight, so we can eat upstairs."

"It's a date." Reluctantly, with a last squeeze of her hand, he headed for the door. "Don't let her run."

"I'll try not to."

Chapter Ten

Upstairs, Bernie barely got the door open before Ren—Jen—was in her arms.

"I'm so sorry. I've caused you so much trouble. You don't deserve this."

Bernie smoothed the hair back from Jen's face and saw her tear-ravaged eyes.

"Honey, it's okay. It's all going to work out."

"No, it isn't," Jen cried. "I've ruined everything."

"Come sit down so we can talk."

They settled on the couch and Jen tucked herself into Bernie's body.

"Now, what is it you think you've ruined?"

"My life. Your life. Everything. I know Mr. Gibson said he wouldn't call anyone, but he has to. That's his job."

"He promised you. And he gave me assurances he would not make any calls without telling you first. I believe him."

"You do? Really?"

Bernie nodded into Jen's head. "I do. He, umm, dug up my past and didn't think any worse of me because of it." Warmth filled her to think of Paul's reaction. He had accepted her just as she was. Having been part of the system, then responsible for her own protection for so long, it was strange to have someone else to talk to about it. Two someones. What a couple of weeks!

Bernie hugged Jen, then moved her away so she could see her face. "Paul has gone back to his place to do more digging into your mother's boyfriend. He wasn't kidding when he said he sensed something was off, Jen. But he couldn't find anything before, and to a certain extent, his hands were tied. He's trying again. Is there anything you know that might help him?"

Jen wrung her hands. "Not really. I wish I did."

"What does this man do for a living?"

"He's a long-haul trucker. He'd be gone for four or five days at a time. Those were the only times I could breathe. He didn't allow Mom to work. She wasn't allowed to leave the house except to go to the grocery store. He had a tracker on her phone, and he'd call her all the time just to be sure she had it with her."

"What an asshole."

"Yeah. The funny thing was, I saw one of his bank statements once. He and Mom had separate accounts. He told Mom he had money. He didn't. Less than $100 in his account."

"He lied to your mother? Any idea why?"

Jen shook her head.

"Okay if I tell Paul this?"

"If you think it will help."

"I also need to give him your bio-dad's name."

Jen hesitated. Bernie stayed quiet, giving her time to sort it all out.

"We have to find him so we can sort out the legalities."

Jen nodded and pulled her ever-ready backpack up on the couch. Digging inside it for a minute, she pulled out a piece of paper and handed it to Bernie.

"My birth certificate."

"Good girl, keeping that with you."

"Figured I might need it someday."

Bernie took a picture of the document, then handed it back to Jen. She attached the pic to a text with the information about the boyfriend, then looked at Jen, her hand paused over the send arrow. "You okay with me sending this to Paul?"

"I guess I don't have much of a choice."

"I trust him."

"I will too, until he proves me wrong."

Bernie tapped the arrow to send. "Let's hope that doesn't happen." *For both our sakes.*

~~~

That night, Paul watched Bernie and Jen as they worked in Bernie's kitchen like a well-oiled machine. He could already tell Bernie liked the girl. She wasn't going to take it well if Jen had to live with someone else. Which was why he'd held off telling them the news until after dinner. Besides, his stomach growled at all the wonderful scents. Was that garlic bread?

"Dinner's ready," Bernie said, carrying a dish in each hand to the table. Jen followed, carrying more.

"Jen did almost all the work."

"No, I didn't. You helped just as much."

They set the dishes down. "Well, if you hadn't done all the prep work and gotten things in the oven, it would be another hour before we ate. Maybe longer."

"You found the recipe. And had the ingredients."

"Only because I run an Italian pizza parlor."

Paul poured sparkling cider for everyone. "Can we all just agree that you both get credit for dinner? It looks fantastic."

His heart swelled when Jen blushed at the compliment. This girl had a tender heart, filled with generosity and goodness. He needed to be very careful how he handled this situation or she'd be jaded for the rest of her life. She should be already. The fact that she'd kept her good heart was a testament to her strength.

The pasta primavera was exceptional. "Wow," Paul said, chewing slowly. "This is fantastic."

"Bernie's recipe."

"But you made it," Bernie said.

"The recipe is great, though I know from experience it's all in the hands of the cook." He smiled at Jen, who blushed. "I have my mother's tried and true recipes and haven't been able to get even one of them to taste like she made them."

"I'd love to try some of them," Jen said. "Mom... didn't feel well a lot, so I did a lot of the cooking. Turns out, I kind of like it."

"Hopefully, you'll get the chance."

That little note of caution killed the mood at the table and Paul mentally kicked himself.

"Is there news?" Bernie asked.

Setting his fork down, Paul took a sip of cider to clear his throat. Both Bernie's and Jen's eyes were guarded. Better to get this out in the open.

"Gavin Thompson is looking for you."

Jen gasped and Bernie gripped her hand.

"I'm not going back to him."

"Let me finish," Paul said. "He's got a private investigator hunting and has run a lot of ads. Willow Bay isn't that far from Vancouver, so until we get this straightened out, you'll need to keep your head down."

"I have been."

"Yet I found you." He paused to let that sink in. "You need to be even more cautious."

"Did you dig into Gavin's past?" Bernie asked.

"I'm working on it. It's weird. I can't seem to find anything past about five years ago. That is highly unusual. Whoever accepted that and okayed his guardianship must have been half asleep."

"So what's next?"

"I don't suppose you might have anything with his fingerprints on it?" Paul asked Jen, who shook her head.

"Then I need to go home." He hated to go. This town,

and the people who lived here, were growing on him. One or two in particular.

With a glance at Bernie, Jen stiffened.

"Just for a couple days," Paul added. "If I can set up a meeting with Gavin, maybe I can get his fingerprints. That's the only way I'm going to be able to dig any further into him."

"You'll tell him where I am."

"I haven't yet, have I?" Paul crouched beside Jen's chair. He disengaged her hand from Bernie's, then took both of them in his. "You trust Bernie, right?"

She nodded.

"Now, I need you to trust me. I won't do anything without talking to you first."

Jen removed her hands from Paul's and locked eyes with Bernie. When the girl turned back to him, he was gratified to find her smiling and nodding.

"Okay," Jen said. "I'll trust you."

Until you prove me wrong, her eyes said.

"Good! I'll leave tomorrow and keep Bernie apprised of how things are going. There's, uh, more news. I think I've found your father."

Jen, who'd resumed eating her dinner, whipped her head up. "You have?"

"Only a paternity test will confirm it, but he fits."

"Who is he? What does he do? Where does he live?" The questions came one right after the other with no breath in between.

Paul laughed, holding up his hands. "Surprisingly, he doesn't live that far away. He's based in Portland. He's a long-haul trucker."

Jen's face fell. "Just like Gavin. Seems my mom had a type."

"Just because they work in the same industry doesn't

mean they are the same type of person."

"Besides," Bernie said, "you said he was an army guy. Your mom wouldn't have known what he'd do when he got out. Not back then."

"Mom never did well on her own. She tended to meet men who wanted to be in control. I guess that's where she felt safe. Until the first bruises, at least." A tear slid down Jen's face.

Paul covered Jen's hand with his own, looking at Bernie, trying to convey the fact that there was more to the story. Bernie caught his meaning and frowned.

"What?" Jen asked, pushing back to glance between them. "No secrets, remember?" She scowled at Paul. "You said you'd tell me everything."

He nodded. He had promised. "All right. Here are the last bits of new information I have. He's married, and I can't find any indication he even knows about you."

Tears filled Jen's eyes. "Proves my theory, then. Mom never told him."

"We can't draw conclusions," Bernie said, giving Jen a reassuring pat. "We don't have enough information." She grabbed dirty plates, set them on the counter, and came back for more. "Do you want to pursue this thing with your bio-dad?"

"We can quite easily," Paul added. He hoped Jen would say yes. Right now, this seemed like the best avenue for her. And it would give them leverage when Gavin tried to get her back under this thumb.

"I—I don't know." Jen chewed on a fingernail.

"How about this," Bernie said. "We'll let Paul work on getting information about that boyfriend of your mother's. The bio-dad thing can be dealt with any time, right?"

Paul agreed.

"So, why not just think about that for a while?" Bernie

said.

Jen's nod was slow to come, but she seemed to perk up. "I think that's the best way to go."

"Good. Now let's get these dishes done, settle in for some mindless television, and forget about life for a while."

After dishes, which neither Jen nor Bernie would let Paul help wash, Jen excused herself. "I think I'm going to put headphones on and zone out."

Bernie gave her a hug. "It's a lot to process."

"Yeah." She nodded. "'Night, Paul. 'Night, Bernie."

They watched her disappear into her room.

"There's a lot of hurt and worry on those shoulders," Bernie said.

"We'll figure it out, all of us together. Do what's best for Jen."

"Until legalities get in the way."

Paul pulled Bernie into his arms, resting his chin on her head as she hugged him. "Yeah."

He tightened his hug. "I like you like this."

"Submissive?"

"Never. Just... amenable."

Bernie chuckled into his chest. "You feel pretty... amenable yourself."

"And getting more so." Just holding her, the attraction blossomed between them.

"We've got a teenager here," Bernie said.

"And I'm a social worker. Probably wouldn't look good if I did what I'd like to do to her pseudo-foster parent in the same apartment."

"Nope." Bernie sighed.

"Want to come back to my place?" He held his breath.

"Not sure that's a good idea, either. We've only just met, and there were some pretty big issues holding us apart. Plus, I don't want to leave Jen."

It was Paul's turn to sigh. After a long moment, he willed his libido to stand down and he stepped back. "Okay, find a mindless television show and we'll neck our way through it."

A shaky laugh told him Bernie felt the same pull he did. "Sounds like a good plan."

"But first— " Paul lowered his head, pausing just before he touched her to revel in the welling of emotions inside him.

Bernie leaned in, closing the distance. Their lips touched. Everything touched, or that's what it felt like. The unfamiliar becoming familiar, the search finding answers. Warmth growing into need. He ran his hands up her back, tangled them in her hair.

Her hands tightened around his neck, pulling him in closer, snuggling up to him, his jeans tight as she ground against him.

When he broke the kiss, they leaned, forehead to forehead, breathing hard.

"Wow," Bernie said.

"Yeah. Wow." Paul had never known a kiss like that. Ever. One kiss had ripped his world from its axis and he free-floated, trying to find some equilibrium. He wasn't sure he ever would.

They sank to the couch. Bernie ran her fingers over his lips.

"These things are dangerous."

"Only with you."

She licked her lips as if trying to capture the essence of his taste and Paul leaned in, kissing her again. He wanted more. He wanted to never stop. She tasted of apples and toothpaste and he was struck by the random wonder at when she'd found time to brush her teeth. Then she nudged him with her tongue and they danced upon waves of desire and sensation.

His hands moved up and down her back, into her hair, around the swell of her breast. Her hands were just as active, un-tucking his t-shirt, slipping underneath, skin-to-skin. He shivered as she ran her hands over the muscles of his back. Down his spine, then up.

His thumb dragged across her nipple, bringing a gasp from her. Paul broke the kiss. "If we keep going, I don't think I'll be able to stop."

"Me, either," Bernie said, breathing hard. "You get to me. In all the best ways."

"I know that feeling." Paul sat back, running a hand through his hair, loving the feel of her hand as she settled it on his chest and tucked in under his arm. Damn, but he wanted to finish this. No, that wasn't the right phrase. He wanted to keep this going for... forever.

The thought surprised him. He'd had relationships in the past, but never once had he thought in terms of the future. It was always comfortable for now with him and whoever he dated. His job, and the aches and pains that went with it, didn't make for good relationships. Not when all he saw was the seedy side of life.

"What are you thinking?" Bernie asked.

"Why?"

"You tensed up."

Paul forced himself to relax. "Sorry, just thinking about the day job."

"Oh, that's flattering."

He pulled her in tighter. "If it helps me keep my hands off you, it's worth it."

She nodded into his chest. "Point taken."

"So, as much as I'd like to take this to a bed—any bed—maybe we'd better find some of that mindless television to focus on."

With a badly exaggerated sigh, Bernie reached for the

remote.

~~~

Jen opened the door to her bedroom around midnight, surprised to see lights still on. She pulled her earbuds out and crept out to the main area.

In the living room, she stopped beside the couch, smiling. Bernie and Paul were sound asleep, sitting with their arms around each other and the TV still on. It was the cutest damn thing she'd ever seen, and it filled Jen with a yearning beyond anything she'd ever felt. This was what family was meant to be. She wondered if her bio-dad's family was like that. Did he have kids? She'd need to ask Paul. Maybe she had sisters and brothers. Jen cocked her head, trying to decide if she liked that idea. Yes. She did.

Clicking off the TV, she killed the lights and went back to bed. Hope had been easing into her ever since that old lady had found her. Hope that she might actually have a future. A family. This was what she wanted.

And she wanted it more than anything else in the world.

Chapter Eleven

Bernie and Jen chopped pizza ingredients in silence. Jen probably had a lot of thinking to do. So did Bernie. She and Paul had woken up at 3 a.m. with cricks in their necks and the TV and lights turned off.

Last night had been... what? Amazing? Stupendous? World-rocking? All of the above. She'd never felt that strong of a pull toward someone before. Granted, it had been a while and she was a bit deprived. Tristan had put her off men. But Paul triggered something in her, a feeling of completeness. He was such a gentle, caring man. They'd barely just met and she felt like she knew him. Understood him. And he understood her, trusted her. She'd never let anyone inside, not like Paul. And she was in serious danger of losing her heart if he changed his mind about them.

He'd gone home for a couple days, which was probably a good thing, though Bernie already missed him. Some distance might help her find her equilibrium. A part of her, the self-sufficient, I-don't-need-anyone person had gone into hiding. That scared her. Two people had become important to her. She needed some perspective.

Never having fallen asleep in front of the TV in a man's arms, she'd had no idea what the protocols were when they woke up. She'd blushed and Paul had chuckled before kissing the life out of her again, then heading home. The only thing Bernie didn't know was how the TV went off. Maybe it died?

"So, you and Paul looked pretty cozy last night," Jen said, recalling Bernie from her thoughts.

Crap. That explained the TV. She should have known. Bernie chose the avenue of least resistance and remained silent, hoping Jen would let it drop. No such luck.

"You seem to be getting along."

"I'm not going to talk about this." Bernie smashed a clove of garlic with more force than necessary, pulverizing it.

"What? About your love life, you mean?"

"I have no love life." Oh, but God, did she wish she had. "Have you decided about your bio-dad?"

"Nice change of topic." Jen's smile disappeared. "Effective, too. And no, I haven't decided yet."

Bernie turned around and leaned against the counter. "What's holding you back?"

"If he doesn't know about me, what will that do to his wife? Maybe he's an asshole like the boyfriend. Or has a lady in every town on his route and I have siblings. Lots of siblings."

"So the knowing might be worse than the not knowing."

"Exactly."

They prepped food for several minutes before Jen spoke again.

"What do you think I should do?"

"I wish I knew." Bernie put the lettuce in the cooler and closed the door. "Honestly, this is something you'll have to decide for yourself. Either way, you're taking a chance."

"I'd like to stay here. Finding him could complicate that."

Bernie paused. The expression on Jen's face told her she'd paused too long.

"You don't want me to stay." Jen plunked the bowl she'd been holding on the counter and whipped off her apron, turning to leave.

"Gonna run?"

"Why not?"

"Because we're trying to help you, and right now, we're the only help you've got."

"Help me out of your hair, you mean."

Oh, yes, Bernie remembered that hurt, when you felt like there wasn't one single person in the entire world who was on your side.

"You going to let me explain why I didn't answer right away?"

"Why? It's the same story all over again. You're siding with the system. With Paul Gibson."

"Hey. I don't deserve that and neither does Paul." Bernie pointed to the stool beside the pizza oven. "Sit."

Jen pursed her lips, then drew them in so tight Bernie could hardly see them. But the kid plopped herself down on the stool.

"I learned a long time ago never to make promises I couldn't keep. I also learned, the hard way, to think before I speak. Taking time to answer you has nothing, I repeat, nothing to do with you. It has everything to do with those two mantras that I try to live by. So don't get your panties in a wad over a few seconds of silence."

Bernie could hear her voice getting louder, and that wasn't what she wanted, so she took a deep breath and clutched the counter behind her. "I want you to know, I'd love to have you stay here. But not illegally, at least not long term. We need to figure out how to do this by the book. And that means this discussion is moot until we have more answers."

Tears filled Jen's eyes. Bernie broke her rule about keeping her distance and pulled the girl into her chest.

"I'm just s-so s-scared."

"I know. I know." She smoothed the kid's hair, her heart filling with emotion to witness Jen's misery. Bernie wanted her to be happy. Needed her to be settled in a good place like she needed air to breathe.

But Jen also needed to cry the crap she'd gone through right out of her life, so Bernie just held her as the flood doors opened. For a time Bernie couldn't gauge, they stood there, rocking back and forth. Eventually, Jen's tears became snuffles and she backed away.

"Feel better?"

"No."

"You will. Don't worry. I'm on your side. So is Paul."

"I guess that means I'm on your side, too?"

Bernie and Jen whirled at the new voice.

"Josh," Bernie said. "I didn't hear you come in."

"So I figured." His blue eyes bored into Bernie, then turned to Jen. He held out his hand. "We haven't met. I'm Josh Morgan."

Jen, who'd been furiously wiping her tears off her face, dried her hands on a towel, then shook Josh's hand.

"This is my niece, Jen, here visiting me from... San Francisco," Bernie said.

"Nice to meet you." Josh looked Bernie's lie straight in the face. "Are you enjoying our oceanside town?"

Jen nodded.

"Why don't you go upstairs and clean up," Bernie said to Jen. "I'll finish prep. Thanks for helping me."

The girl's jerky nod showed her fear as she slid past Josh. With a "later" and a wave, she was out the door. Both Josh and Bernie turned to the window as heavy footfalls raced up the stairs.

Josh chuckled. "She couldn't get out of here fast enough."

Bernie shrugged. "She's got her reasons."

"Anything to do with the fact that you don't have any siblings?"

Damn. Mantra number three: never lie to your best friend.

Bernie chose not to answer. Instead, she hung up Jen's apron, put a lid on the pungent, grated cheese, and got the food back in the cooler.

"She's the runaway that guy's been looking for, right?"

"What if she is?"

"Crap." Josh ran his hands through his hair. "I'm the mayor, Bern. I am legally bound to follow the rules."

"Then you shouldn't walk into businesses before they are open for the day."

He shook his head. "What have you gotten yourself into?"

"Look, it's no big deal. She needs some help, is all."

"She needs to be with the folks who can figure out the best thing for her. This is a child, Bernie. A teenager. Not some mangy pup on the street you can feed and find a home for."

"I know that. But I can help her. God, Josh, you should have seen how scared she was when she first got here."

"First got here?"

Double damn. Mantra number two: think before you speak.

"I'm going to call that guy. There's no choice. I'm sorry, Bernie."

Bernie sank onto the stool. No way could she explain that Paul knew and was helping them. He could lose his job. "You don't have to call him."

"Yes, I do. This is beyond anything we can take care of."

"She needs help." Bernie got up and clutched Josh's arms. "And time. Please. Just give us a little time to sort this out."

Josh looked long and hard at Bernie and she let him see it all. The fear, the worry, the need to help Jen. "You're afraid for her, aren't you?"

"Yes. Very."

"You never told me what your life was like before you came to Willow Bay," Josh said, his voice gentle. "Is that your past? Something like this girl's?"

Unable to say the words, she nodded.

"Damn, Bern." Josh pulled her in for a quick hug, then paced the kitchen.

"All right. I'll give you two days. If you don't have some sort of resolution by then, I'm calling that guy."

"Thank you, Josh. I'm being straight with you. I think this will work out and Jen will be in a better situation because of it. We just need time."

"Don't take too long. My loyalty is to you, and if I think you'll be hurt by this, I'll take action."

Bernie smiled. This kind of big-brother love was a wonderful thing that had been sorely lacking during her childhood. "How's Dana?"

"The shop's been really busy, which is good. And she's knee-deep in wedding stuff."

"You're helping her, right?"

"Of course."

"Why don't I believe that?"

"I do every single thing she asks me to do in a timely manner and I offer opinions when asked. Honestly, Dana and I in front of a judge would be perfect for me, but she wants to include the town. So I'm on board."

"Good. You both deserve this celebration."

"Yeah." Josh glanced at his phone. "Well, I'd better get back to the office. The kickoff meeting for the first annual Beer and Chowder festival starts soon."

"Oooh, I forgot. I was going to go to that."

"I'll let you know how it goes. You've got enough to worry about." With a glance at the ceiling, Josh shook his head and headed for the door.

"Hey, did you come by for something?"

"Oh, yeah. Dana wants pizza tonight. The usual, with everything. Can I swing by around seven and pick it up?"

Josh's fiancé sure liked her pizza. Bernie chuckled. "Sure. I'll have it ready."

"Thanks." With a wave of his hand, Josh was out the door.

Bernie's smile disappeared and she headed straight upstairs to check on Jen. Sure enough, the place was empty and all Jen's stuff was gone. Bernie rushed outside and down the stairs to find Gladys had the girl—who was in her running clothes, backpack in hand—by the ear again.

"Caught this one rushing out. Figured I'd better ask if everything you own is still there." She let go of Jen, who stood there rubbing her ear.

"She wouldn't steal from me, Gladys, but I'm glad you stopped her. We still have some things to work out."

"Well, you need any muscle, you let me know." Gladys flexed an arm that had more clothes covering it than muscle. "I've still got ways to get things done."

"Thanks." She eyed Gladys, who looked a little peaked. "You all right? You need anything? Food? A place to stay?" If she said yes to that last one, Bernie would have to hang a "home for the homeless" sign out.

"I'm fine." Gladys waved her hand. "I'll leave the girl with you."

"Yes. And again, thanks." Bernie grabbed Jen's backpack and stomped to one of two outdoor tables, plopping down.

"Sit."

Jen glared at her.

"Sit down, Jen."

With sullen slowness, Jen sat across from Bernie. Close enough to talk, far enough to get a head start if she ran. She reached for her pack.

"Leave it."

She grabbed hold of the strap, wrapping it around her

wrist, but she'd didn't move it. That's street sense, always keeping a hand on your pack. Bernie hated that Jen had learned to keep her possessions close.

"Don't leave."

"I have to," Jen said. "That guy will tell on us. And I can't go back. Plus, I'm putting everything you've worked for in jeopardy."

"How do you figure that?"

"You're breaking the law having me here. I'm not going to let my problems become bigger ones for you."

Bernie leaned forward. "My problems aren't bigger because of you. Maybe a bit more complicated, but not bigger."

"Now, that guy knows about me. All he needs to do is mention it to one person, who'll mention it to another, and bam! I'm back in hell with Mom's boyfriend."

"First of all, I'll run with you before I let you go back to that ass. And Josh won't tell. I arrived in Willow Bay a couple years before Josh planted himself here. Got a job at this pizza place and worked hard, saving my money. Bought the place about a year after I met Josh, when the owner retired. And Josh was the first person in the door when I renamed it. We've been best friends ever since. He's the one person in the world I can count on no matter what. And he won't give you up." At least, not for forty-eight hours.

"Me being here, it's not good for you. I'm going to screw things up for you if I stay."

The girl clutched the pack strap so tight, Bernie thought she might rip it, so she reached across, unthreaded Jen's fingers from around the strap, and held her hand between her own two, warming them both. "You are not screwing things up for me. I like my life complicated, apparently. And I can deal with that. Please. Give Paul a chance to do some digging. Decide about your bio-dad. Let's resolve your situation. That will uncomplicate things for all of us."

Jen's lips trembled. Her hand shook as Bernie cocooned it.

"I—I don't want to leave."

"Then don't. Stay. Please. Give Paul and me a chance to help you sort this out."

The time it took for Jen to make a decision stretched out until Bernie wanted to scream. Finally, in a voice so quiet the far-off ocean roar almost drowned it out, Bernie got her answer.

"All right."

Letting out a huge breath of relief, Bernie let go, then patted Jen's hand. "Good. Now how about we get the rest of the prep done. We open in less than an hour."

"'Kay. I'll take my bag upstairs and be down in a minute."

Bernie watched her head up the stairs, then went inside, hoping the kid meant what she'd said. Somehow, Jen had gotten under her skin. She cared about what happened to her. When the door opened and Jen walked in, back in t-shirt and jeans. Bernie's world righted itself.

"Okay. Enough drama," she said. "Back to work."

~~~

Paul felt like he'd been gone weeks, but only two days had passed. He knew a bit more about Jen's situation but hadn't wanted to talk about it on the phone. Calling Bernie each night had left him wanting so much more than just phone contact, and he'd selfishly spent the time getting to know her. But now they had some decisions to make. He'd met with Gavin and came away feeling like he needed a shower. The man had been surly and uncommunicative, but had let Paul in.

"What's this all about? Have you found the girl yet?"

Paul had worked hard to keep from glancing at the

stairs, and the floor at the bottom of them, where Jen's mother had been found.

"She's not back in the system yet," Paul said, trying hard not to lie. "I was hoping you might be able to think of something, anything that might help find Jen."

"Like what?" Gavin plopped down in a recliner so old that it can't slightly to the left. He'd apparently muted the television, but that didn't keep him from watching it while Paul was there. He wore a t-shirt with the sleeves torn off and the amount of muscle the man had almost intimidated Paul.

"If you could remember anything she liked to do. Hobbies, etc."

"How am I supposed to know that? She's a kid. I didn't follow her around."

"Maybe you took her shopping or bought her supplies?"

"Her mother did that. God rest her soul."

"Yes. I'm so sorry for your loss."

"Yeah," the guy grunted.

"We already have her known friends. Is there anything you can tell us, anything at all? Is there any art that she did you can show us?"

"Might be a few pictures she drew. Not sure how that can help." But he climbed out of the recliner. "Be right back."

While he was gone, Paul looked around for something that might have prints. There were two empty beer bottles beside the recliner. Glancing at the doorway, Paul scooped one up and put it in the bag he carried in his satchel, hoping Gavin wouldn't miss an empty bottle.

Gavin returned with two pieces of paper. "I grabbed these from the girl's room."

Paul looked at them. A dragon painting, really well done, and a unicorn. Jen had talent."

"Thank you. This might give me some ideas. Can I take them with me?"

"Not sure how they can help, but sure."

"Great. I'll get out of your hair now."

Gavin followed Paul to the front door and let him out. "Just see that you get the girl back to me as soon as possible. My patience is growing thin."

Paul had left there with no more information than when he'd arrived. But he'd gotten the guy's fingerprints and that had opened up a whole new set of problems. At first, Paul couldn't decide if he should tell Jen everything or not. With his promise to the kid hanging over his head, he'd chosen to hold off on doing anything until he talked to her and Bernie, which meant his back was against the wall. He had to tell her all of it.

Back at the office, his boss had told him to wrap the case up and get back to work. A mound of files sat on his desk. Guilt swamped him. So many cases needed his attention. So many kids needed help. It overwhelmed him.

When he pulled into Willow Bay, something inside him eased. Life moved slowly here, and the pace had settled in his heart. He wanted this but wasn't sure he could have it with all the work waiting for him. He worked days, nights, weekends, whatever was required. It had never bothered him before. At least, he hadn't thought it bothered him. But now, he was tired. Overworked. For the first time in years, he wanted to have a life of his own and not be married to the job.

Square Peg came into view and improved his attitude. Paul wanted this. He wanted a life outside of work. He left everything in the car. The place didn't open for a couple hours yet, but he knew they'd be getting ready and the doors were unlocked. Stepping inside the restaurant, he took a deep, calming breath. It smelled like Italian spices and tomato sauce. Like home.

Bernie came out of the kitchen wiping her hands on a towel. "Paul!" She launched herself around the counter and into his open arms. He tucked into her neck, smelling the dough she'd been kneading, feeling the way her soft body molded to his. God, he'd fallen deep off the edge. As she welcomed him with a kiss, he didn't mind that abyss one bit.

He could see Jen watching from the kitchen doorway. A smile lit her face for Bernie's happiness but tension showed in her shoulders and stance. Paul waved her over.

"Okay if I hug you?"

"Y-yes," Jen said.

He pulled her in, keeping it light. "I've missed you. Both of you."

Jen's smiled widened. It melted Paul's heart when she hugged him back.

When they pulled apart, Bernie looked at him. "You've brought news."

"I have. I'm not sure we shouldn't wait until tonight to go over it all, though."

"No." Jen's voice was resolute, so they sat down at one of the tables.

"First, your biological father."

Jen leaned forward.

"He's married, but they don't have any kids. Looks like she wasn't able to. He earns a solid wage doing long-haul trucking."

"And has a woman in every town, I bet," Jen said.

"I don't get that impression. He and his wife have been married for ten years, so you came along before that. I don't think he'd even met her when he knew your mom. I'm not sure why he and your mom didn't work out, but unless my radar is completely screwed up, I don't think he knows about you. Have you decided if you want to reach out to him?"

"I... "

"Be honest, Jen," Bernie said. "You can talk to us. I think we've proven our ability to keep your secrets."

"It's not about secrets. I'm worried about how he'll react. And... I want to stay here. I'm happy here. With you."

Bernie reached over and tucked a stray hair behind Jen's ear. "I know, honey. If we can work that out, we will. But you know my requirement."

"It has to be legal."

"And if the courts find out about your bio-dad, they'll want to reach out to him."

"Yeah." Jen looked at Paul. "Can you reach out to him?"

"On your behalf? Certainly."

She took a deep breath. "Okay. Do it."

"I will call him after we're done here. Actually," Paul swallowed the bile in his throat. "I think Gavin is the bigger issue."

"Why?" Bernie asked, frowning.

"I ran his prints. His name's not Gavin Thompson. I'm not certain what his name is, he's had so many aliases. Are you sure you want to hear this?" Paul watched Jen closely. She was tense, but not closed off. She nodded.

"He's been married several times, under different names. And, each time, his wife died in what I can only call suspicious circumstances."

Jen leaped up. "I knew it! I absolutely knew it. And I tried to tell the coroner, the police, you." She turned accusing eyes on Paul.

"I should have listened," he said honestly, feeling like a heel.

"Correct."

"All right, stop it," Bernie said. "That's water under the bridge. Moving forward, we need a plan and the two of you at opposite corners of the ring won't help one bit."

"You're right, Bern." Paul turned to Jen. "I'm sorry. I should have listened."

It took a few moments. The internal war skewing her facial features would have been comical if the situation wasn't so serious.

"Apology accepted," Jen said, sitting down. "Just don't do it again."

"I hope I won't, but I give you permission to call me on it if I ever do."

She nodded.

"There's one more thing. Jen, did you know your mother had a will?"

"No."

"She did. She left the house and what little money she had to you."

"Not to Gavin?"

Paul shook his head.

"But he's still living in the house."

"I know. And that may be why he's trying so hard to find you. I checked with your mother's bank. He's tried to access her funds but the bank won't let him."

"That asshole," Jen said.

"Hey," Bernie piped in. "Language."

Jen made a face but kept her opinion to herself.

"So what's the plan, then?" Bernie asked. "Oh, I should tell you. Josh, the guy you met on the beach? He knows about Jen."

"How did that happen?"

"He's a good friend and stopped in before hours the day after you left. We were in the kitchen prepping food." Bernie shrugged.

Josh was a good friend? How good?

"He's Willow Bay's mayor," Bernie said.

"I know. And that might complicate things, but... I think

it's time to bring in the authorities anyhow."

"Why?" Jen asked. "Nothing's been resolved. They'll take me away."

"I'm hopeful that my recommendation will get them behind an emergency foster-parent application for Bernie."

Bernie started to speak but Paul forestalled her with his hand. "I went over your file again. When you cleared things up, you did it right. There's nothing in there that should keep you from being an authorized foster parent."

Bernie paused and she and Jen looked at each other, then both burst out laughing.

"Is there something I'm missing?" Paul said, enjoying the happiness on their faces.

"We had this same conversation before you got here, and my pregnant pause almost derailed us." Bernie swiped at an eye. "For the record, yes, I'd love to become Jen's foster parent. The only qualification I have is that it be legal, not under the table."

"Too late for that."

"Well, legal as soon as possible."

"Okay, then. Jen, I think we should talk to the local authorities. I brought my research with me and would like to make them aware of the situation."

Trepidation widened her eyes.

"I recognize there's some risk here, but we're already going to reach out to your biological father. Might as well get it all out in the open."

"What about Gavin?" Jen asked.

"He's going to find you sooner or later. At least this way, we'll have more people watching out and the ability to run things through the courts instead of him just showing up and demanding you go home with him."

"I could call Josh and ask him to bring the sheriff by after closing tonight, or tomorrow morning," Bernie said.

"Josh will be relieved to find out we're going public, anyhow. I don't want to string him along for too long."

More about this Josh guy? He'd seemed nice enough when Paul had met him on the beach. A runner. Paul didn't have time to run. Bernie seemed to think about him a lot and Paul couldn't stop the thought from popping into his head. *Just who was she stringing along?*

"Tonight or tomorrow will be fine with me. I'm at your disposal." With his gaze focused on Bernie, he hoped she'd understand he wanted time with them, with her.

Bernie reached over and squeezed his hand, then stood up. "We open soon." She had a very gratifying apologetic look on her face. "For now, that means you, Jen, better head upstairs."

"All right," Jen said. "You'll let me know when you hear anything, won't you Paul?"

"Definitely."

"And I want to be involved in the meeting with the sheriff."

"Of course," Paul and Bernie said together. They smiled at each other, then Paul stood, came around the table, and pulled Bernie into his arms.

"Okay, then. I guess I'll give you two a moment of privacy." Jen chuckled as she headed for the door. "Don't do anything I wouldn't do."

"Can't," Bernie hollered after her. "No time."

Jen's chuckles wafted behind her as she headed upstairs.

As soon as the door upstairs closed, Paul leaned into Bernie. "Been waiting too long to do this." His lips touched hers and the last piece of his future fell into place.

Bernie leaned into him, increasing the depth of their kiss. Paul felt his world open up. Together, they were perfect. With Bernie's caring heart, together they could do anything, help kids, whatever they wanted. The hole Paul hadn't known he had inside him filled with all the emotion he'd kept locked up for so many years. Waiting for this. For her. His soul mate.

Bernie broke the kiss and backed up a step. "I don't think," she said through deep breaths, "you know what you do to me."

Paul pulled her in, pressing her close. "I think you can feel exactly what you do to me." He leaned in to kiss her again, but Bernie put a hand to his lips.

"I open in ten minutes."

"Damn," Paul said, running his hands through his short hair. "I forgot. That quickly. That's what you do to me."

"As gratifying as that is, I have some more prep work to do." She nudged him toward the door. "And a phone call to make."

"Okay. But later, we're going to finish this... discussion."

"I look forward to it."

He kissed her, then reluctantly left for his still-rented condo.

~~~

"What the hell is all this?"

Paul switched his cell to speaker so his boss's voice wouldn't sound so shrill. He set it on the small dining table and looked out at the ocean waves, searching for calm, as he answered.

"The email I sent you? It's all my research into Jennifer Moore's case."

"Fingerprint costs, police reports? This is above and beyond what we do. We find these kids and place them where the courts tell us to. You're causing me stress on a Saturday, Gibson."

Place them. Like dinnerware. Paul cringed at the words.

"It was necessary in this case."

"We don't have the money to spend on this kind of shit,

Paul. You're supposed to get approval, and I sure as hell don't remember approving all this."

"Look what I found out. Read it, Randy. We can't send her back to that legal guardian. He's got a rough history, and it's obvious he doesn't want her out of love. He wants her because her mother left everything to Jen and Gavin can only get at it through her."

"That's not our problem, and this isn't the first time you've been told this. You've been in the meetings, Paul. A lot of kids need help. We don't have the time or the resources to deal with this."

"Your predecessor would have— "

"I don't give a rat's ass what she would have done. We have less money now than we did five years ago, and more cases. I'm here to balance the budget and you're making my life very difficult. There's nothing here we can use to prove she'd be at risk with him. Bring the girl back, turn her over to her legal guardian, then you are off this case. You hear me?"

Paul chose to withhold comment because he might finally tell his boss what he really thought.

"Don't mess with me on this, Paul. I expect you in my office tomorrow morning, sans girl. And if you don't follow orders, you can clear out your desk. Got it?"

"Got it, sir." Paul clenched his teeth to keep from saying any more. If he did, he wouldn't need to clean out his desk. Randy would light it on fire.

Punching the end button on his cell, Paul walked to the patio to listen to the quiet roar of ocean waves and let the damp, salty air calm him. He couldn't do it anymore. He couldn't live by rules designed to protect everyone but those who need protection the most. Someone always lost out. He'd joined CPS to help kids, but instead, he only saw the dirty, seedy, ugly side of life. Well, not always. There were bright spots, like Jen. Then there were the Georgies. Blood everywhere. God, why couldn't he focus on the ones he'd helped, not the ones he lost?

This job had worn him out. He wanted to find something better to do with his passion for helping kids. Something happier. He just didn't know what that could be. One thing was certain. He wouldn't be in the office tomorrow morning. Bernie had texted him. Josh and the sheriff would be at Square Peg at 9 a.m. and by God, Paul would be there, too, with Bernie and Jen. The two of them meant more to him than his dead-end job. He needed to see this through the right way.

Paul headed for his empty bed, wishing it wasn't. And praying the future would offer the right kind of answers.

One thing was certain. Tomorrow was going to be a lot harder than today.

Chapter Twelve

When Sheriff Jackson Smith and Josh Morgan arrived at the restaurant the next morning, Bernie figured they weren't expecting to see three such tense, serious people. Bernie's nerves were about fried, and Jen had nearly bolted again this morning.

"Hey, Josh. Hey, Jackson," Bernie said, only having to clear her throat once.

Jackson held something in his arms. As he came further into the restaurant, Bernie saw it was a puppy. Golden lab, by the looks of it.

Jen saw it at the same time as Bernie and squealed. Without hesitation, she went straight to Jackson. "Can I pet him?" she asked.

"You can hold him if you'd like," Jackson said, handing the puppy over with a smile.

Fully aware that she was the town's stray-homer, Bernie mock-glared at Jackson. "Seriously, you bring me a stray when you know there's a kid here?"

The sheriff shrugged, his grin firmly in place. "I never know when these are going to show up. Betty Johnson brought him in. Said he'd been hanging around their hardware store for a couple days. No collar, no chip."

Jen had settled on the floor with the puppy and already, Bernie could see the bond forming. "Low blow, Jackson. I won't forget this."

He laughed, holding his hands up. Then, with his voice lowered, he added, "I thought your stray could use a friend."

Bernie's attitude melted away. Jackson was right. Jen could use a friend, and these two were fast becoming that. She had some for strays, but it looked like they'd be making a trip to get more.

Paul shook hands with both men. It struck Bernie how comfortable he was around people. Where you came from or what you looked like didn't matter to Paul Gibson. He accepted everyone. She fell a little more for him in that instant. Her fleeting thought about how bad it was going to hurt when he went home for good disappeared with Jackson's question.

"So, what's up with the kid?"

Bernie indicated they should all sit. Once they did, Paul opened his mouth to speak, but Bernie shushed him with a small wave. She turned to Jen, who sat next to her, puppy in arms, and waited.

"I'm—I'm a runaway, and I'm scared to death to go back to the guy who's been assigned legal guardianship." The words came out like a surprise burst of wind, all at once, then stopped just as suddenly.

Even Josh held his breath as they waited for Jackson's reaction.

"That's one hell of an opening line, young lady."

"I found her," Gladys said, walking in and sitting down even though she hadn't been invited. No one told her to leave. Bernie smiled as she kept on talking. "I thought she was up to no good, rustling around in the bushes beside the restaurant. So I've been watching her. Turns out, she's a decent kid. Works hard."

Gladys looked at Bernie, who nodded her head.

"She is. She's been helping me here and my apartment's never been so clean. She cooks, too."

"She's got a good head on her shoulders," Gladys said. "Coulda run several times, from what I've seen. She knows this is a good place and it looks like she's decided to stick it out, thick or thin." Turning to Jen, she laid a wrinkled hand on the girl's arm. "I'm sorry if I gave you the impression I didn't think much of you. People have to earn respect, and, from what I see and hear, you've earned mine. Jackson," she said, turning to the sheriff. "You'd better do the right thing for this girl or you'll have me to reckon with."

"Got it, Miss Gladys. I'll try my best."

With that assurance, Gladys patted him on the cheek, waved goodbye, and was out the door, pushing her shopping cart along the road to wherever she chose.

"Boy, that woman has you whipped," Josh said.

"Don't kid yourself, mayor," Jackson flipped back. "She's the one who really runs this town."

"Don't I know it."

"Okay, back to business," Jackson said. "I think I'd better hear this story from the beginning."

Paul and Bernie looked at each other, then Bernie told the story from the day she met Jen until Paul found out she was here. Jackson didn't ask any questions, even when Jen chimed in with what had happened and why she'd run. Paul brought up the tail end of the story with what he'd found out and what his boss had ordered him to do.

Then they waited. Jackson got up and walked around the restaurant, looking at Jen and the dog with each pass of the table. Finally, he stopped by Josh's chair. "You don't give me easy problems to solve, mayor."

"Yeah. Sorry about that. Difficult seems to find us here in Willow Bay."

Jackson sat down, cupping a fist into the other hand like a hip socket. "Where are things at with the biological father?"

"I called and left a message, but I haven't heard back," Paul said.

"Did you say why you were calling?" Jen asked.

"No. Didn't want to leave that in a message."

"Well," Jackson broke in. "The law says I should take Jen into custody until she can be remanded to the proper authorities. Seems to me, you're the proper authority, right, Paul?"

"That's what my credentials say."

Bernie wondered at Paul's frown. Was his job in jeopardy?

"Then I'm inclined to let Jen stay in your custody until we can sort this thing out."

"Woohoo!" Jen and Bernie both whooped, startling the puppy, who yelped. Jen sank back down into her seat, cooing to the little guy, who licked her face with his pink tongue.

"But— " Jackson put on his sternest face, the one Bernie had seen him use when teenagers were planning to toilet paper the principal's house. "You run, young woman, and I'll be the one searching for you. You follow orders from Paul and Bernie. I hear you're not toeing the line, I'll fix up a jail cell for you until we can figure out what to do."

Josh and Bernie both coughed and covered their mouths to hide their grins. Jackson was a great sheriff but was so much more bark than bite. Still, he got Jen's attention. She nodded her head emphatically.

"Yes, sir. I'll tow the rope, sir. I promise."

"All right. I think that settles things for now. I want to do some checking into this Gavin character." Jackson stood and shook hands with everyone. "Let me know when you hear from the biological father. I want to know what he says."

"Don't we all," Bernie said.

Bernie watched him leave, all the tension draining from her body as she slumped against the table. Paul put a reassuring arm around her as Jen slid off the chair and turned her attention back to the puppy.

"What should we call him?" Jen asked.

After she gave a pleading look to Paul, Bernie let out a big sigh. "I guess I own a dog." She turned to Jen. "Walking him, cleaning up after him, feeding him, and naming him are all your responsibility. Got it?"

More emphatic nods. "I think I'll call him Juniper."

"Why Juniper?"

"My mom had a dog growing up that she used to talk about. His name was Juniper."

Tears stung at Bernie's eyes. "Okay, then. Juniper it is. You know where the pet supplies are. Go get what you need to set him up in the apartment." Bernie sniffed. "And he'll need a bath. Right away. I'll make a vet appointment later so we can get him checked out."

"Yippee!" Jen cried, hugging the puppy tight and rocking back and forth like she'd just found her best friend. She set the puppy down and stood. "Come on, Juniper!" She raced to the back of the building, the puppy following happily at her heels.

"Oh, Lordy, what have I done?" Bernie said.

"Looks like you've taken on a teenager and a dog," Josh said, laughing.

"And a boyfriend," Paul added, putting his arm around her shoulders.

Josh's eyebrows raised and Bernie tried to scowl at him, but happiness turned her lips upward instead.

"Good for you all," Josh said, his grin widening. "Well, I guess this thing with Jen is all out in the open now," he added. "Time for me to go help Dana open the shop, then get on with my own work."

"I'll walk you out," Paul said. "I have a question I want to ask you."

Bernie watched them talking outside, more grateful than she could ever imagine that Paul had come into her life. No more hiding. Not for Jen, not for her.

Jen came back, the puppy still following along. "I can't find a collar that will fit him."

Out of the corner of her eye, Bernie saw Josh drive off and Paul answer his phone. He glanced inside, then leaned against a post, talking to whoever was on the phone. Maybe it was the bio-dad.

"Come on. I'll see if we can adapt something until we can get to a store."

A few minutes later, Paul joined them, leaning against the door frame of the storage room. Bernie couldn't tell how the call had gone. The man had way too good of a poker face, damn it.

"We found a collar for Juniper!" Jen said to him. "But he's going to grow out of it fast, Bernie says." Jen bounced around like a regular teenager in her zeal.

"That's great. Ummm, we need to talk."

From uber-excited to frozen in place. In a split second. That's all it took for Jen to figure it out. "You talked to my bio-dad."

"I did." Paul glanced at Bernie. "Maybe we should talk in private, Jen?"

That hurt. Big time. Bernie almost put a hand to her heart to stop the bleeding.

"Whatever you have to say to me, you can say to Bernie."

"Okay. Bernie, I'm sorry. I didn't want to have to say that, but for as long as I'm in my official capacity and with nothing quite legal yet, I needed Jen's permission for you to be in on this conversation."

That made things better. A little bit. Though what he meant with that "for as long as" thing bothered her. Just how bad was it at work for him?

"Want to sit down?" Paul asked Jen.

"I've been sitting all morning, it seems like. Just spit it out." Her shoulders slumped as if she could feel the bad news already weighing them down.

"All right." Paul cleared his throat. "He had no idea about you, Jen."

"None?"

"Not a clue. He was astonished."

"And he doesn't need a teenager in his life, right? Another deadbeat bio-dad, nothing special here." Jen dropped onto a crate.

Paul squatted in front of her and lifted her chin. "He wants to meet you."

The pain was back somewhere in the vicinity of Bernie's heart. She was so glad for Jen that her bio-dad wanted to meet her, but the flip side... How could Bernie, who never got attached, have taken this kid into her heart so easily? Damn, but it would be hard to give her up. She'd do it if Jen wanted it, but... damn.

"Yeah, probably wants to figure out how he can use me, too."

"No. At least, that's not the impression I get."

"You're just making it easy on me."

Jen pulled her jaw out of Paul's hand, holding the puppy tight in her arms, in full-on pout mode.

"He was at home when he called me. Said he was going to talk to his wife as soon as he got off the phone and they would plan to be here tomorrow."

"Tomorrow? Like in... tomorrow?"

Even from Bernie's standing position, she could see the hit of hope in Jen's eyes. Quick, but there.

"You told him about Mom's money, right?"

Paul shook his head. "He doesn't know anything except he remembers your mother fondly. I'd like him to tell you the rest of the story himself, but Jen?"

She stared at him.

"I'm a pretty good judge of character and I think he's a stand-up guy."

Paul's phone beeped and he looked down and smiled. "That was fast. They'd like to meet you here at the restaurant at noon tomorrow. Both of them. You okay with that?" Paul kept his fingers poised over the phone.

Jen looked at Bernie. "Are we okay with that?"

"I think a meeting is a good idea," Bernie said slowly.

"Okay, then. Let's do it."

Bernie watched Paul tap out a response, her feelings mixed. Her heart told her that this was a good thing for Jen. That finally, the cogs of her life would start falling into place. Selfishly, though, Bernie didn't want things to change. She wanted Jen to stay with her, to not be alone anymore. Though whether that last thought belonged to Jen or Bernie herself... Bernie had gone from a lifelong solo act to a family and, suddenly, she didn't want to lose that.

"All right. We're set," Paul said.

Jen nodded, then hid her face in the puppy with her eyes closed. "I can't believe this. I, uh, don't know what to think. I think I'll go upstairs and write in my journal."

Paul raised an eyebrow as she left.

"I gave her an empty one a couple days ago and said it was a great way to sort out your thoughts. Turns out, she already knew. That go-bag of hers has a couple of full journals in it."

"That's a really good idea." Paul cocked his head. "Do you have journals?"

"I'm not going to answer that." She did, not that anyone would ever be allowed to read them. Bernie had almost burned them to ash multiple times. Too much pain lay within those pages. Too many hurts that she'd fought to get past.

Paul pulled her into his arms and kissed her, a quick, promising kiss. "Someday, you're going to have to tell me about your past."

"Not anytime soon." Too much pain surrounded those

years. Bernie didn't dredge them up any more than she absolutely had to.

"I've got a surprise for you," Paul said.

No one in Bernie's entire life had ever surprised her. At least, not a happy surprise. She eyed Paul with wary eyes.

He smoothed a hand across her forehead. "It's a good surprise. The restaurant's closed today, so you and I are going out tonight. On an official date."

"But we've got Jen."

"Josh and Dana are taking Jen home with them overnight. Josh said Juniper could come play with their scruff of a dog. Jen will like that, and hopefully not mind the babysitter idea."

"I don't know. A lot has happened today and she's pretty fragile."

"Jen? Fragile? That girl's got your kind of tough in her."

His hand brushed along her hair, sending thrills through her body.

"I want some time, just you and me," he said. "I think we've got something special growing here and I want to test those waters."

"A—all right," Bernie said, aware of how breathless she sounded.

"Great." Paul kissed her again, then backed up. "I'll pick you up at six."

Before she could ask where they were going, he was out the door. Bernie stood there for a long time, fingers to lips, trying to sort out her emotions. She tingled with excitement, but it was tinged with fear. She'd let two people into her life and now cared deeply for both of them.

If Paul left her...

If Jen left...

Bernie might never recover.

~~~

"I think you should wear this," Jen said, pulling a flared and flowery summer dress out of Bernie's closet.

The only dress Bernie owned, she'd bought it on a whim. "That's not a dress for a date. That's for weddings, like Josh and Dana's next month."

"It's perfectly fine for a date."

"Not in May in a northern oceanside town."

"Well, you don't have any other dresses in here."

"Why do I have to wear a dress anyhow? It's just a date."

Jen threw herself dramatically backward onto Bernie's bed, causing Juniper to jump. The girl grabbed the pup and snuggled him, shaking her head at Bernie. "It's never *just* a date, especially not when it's the *first* date."

"Paul and I have been getting to know each other for days now. It's not like we haven't talked. This isn't a first date." The butterflies in Bernie's stomach belied that statement. She clutched her abdomen, wondering if she'd lose lunch while getting ready for dinner.

"Where's he taking you?"

"I don't know." *Damn it.* Bernie didn't like surprises. She normally didn't walk into things without knowing what to expect. She'd been knocked off-kilter and it was all Paul Gibson's fault. Maybe she should cancel. The butterflies in her stomach became bees, buzzing against the walls, aggravating her further.

Who was she kidding? She didn't want to cancel. She wanted time with Paul. He'd become important to her in so many ways. The whole thing with Jen had proven he's a good man. His handsome face and caring blue eyes pulled at Bernie like an undertow. His arms had surrounded her with a warmth and kindness she'd never known before. She was falling hard and there wasn't a thing she could do about it. Not that she wanted to.

So, she was going on this date. And that meant she

needed something to wear. Bernie reached in and pulled out the skinny jeans she rarely wore, with just enough elastic to fit like a glove.

"Yesssssss," Jen said, setting the puppy back in his bed so she could root through Bernie's closet some more. "Now we need a top and some killer heels.

Bernie shook her head. "I'll kill myself if I wear heels."

"Well, shoot, you don't have any. And geesh, Bern, do you own anything besides t-shirts?"

"Never needed anything else before." She sank to the bed. Maybe they could go shopping. They had three hours until Paul picked her up. There wasn't much here in town, though, and it was forty-five minutes to the nearest shopping mall. The downfall of living in a small town. The hardware store was the biggest shopping venue.

"You have friends here, right?"

"I'm friends with the whole town."

"Then call one of them. Borrow something."

Could she? Dana might loan her something. They were pretty close in size.

"All right. I'll call Josh's fiancé'."

Ten minutes later, they were heading out in Bernie's old, orange, dependable Volvo, with Jen's overnight bag and the new puppy in the back seat.

"Gosh, it feels good to be out and about," Jen said.

"No more hiding." The smile on Jen's face made Bernie so happy.

"I sure hope not. I'm not cut out for street living."

"Nobody is, kid." Nobody should ever be.

They walked into the Ta-ngerine Treasures Gift Shop and Jen's face lit up. "This place is awesome!"

Dana's dog, Duffy, began racing around Juniper. Before long, they were rolling around on the floor, growling and playing.

After Bernie introduced Dana, Jen asked if she could look around.

"Sure. Go ahead." Dana turned to Bernie. "So, you need a date outfit, eh?"

Bernie's cheeks grew hot. *Damn it.* "Well, uh, yeah, I guess so."

"With that cute social worker?"

"How do you know he's cute?"

"Josh came home railing about some guy who'd tipped his hat in your direction. Said he was good-looking, but he didn't think he was good enough for you."

"Paul is the nicest, kindest, most generous man I've ever met. He's more than good enough for me. And yes, he's very handsome."

"Don't get your hackles up. You and Josh have been friends for a long time and he's pretty protective of his friends."

"I know." Bernie took a breath and tried to relax. "I'm just keyed up."

"I get that. Come on, let's see what I've got that you can wear."

"You've still got clothes here? I thought you were living at Josh's place."

"They are taping and texturing the entire house this week, so we've moved back into my little back apartment here. Easier than dealing with the dust."

"I can understand that. But are you sure you can watch Jen? Might be crazy with a kid and a puppy back there. Maybe this was a bad idea."

"Uh uh." Dana wagged her finger back and forth. "You don't get out of this date that easily. We've got an air mattress, a TV with some kid-appropriate movies laid out, and lots of popcorn. We'll be fine." Dana eyed Bernie up and down. "So, you mentioned jeans. Did you bring them with you?"

Bernie held them up.

"Great. Change into them and we'll see what goes best. Jen?"

"Yes?" She barely looked away from the display of journals she'd found.

"We'll be in back. Let me know if any customers come in."

"Will do!"

"Thanks," Bernie said to Dana as they headed for the small back apartment.

"For what?"

"For trusting Jen."

"You trust her, so I trust her. Now come on. No more delays. You need a date outfit."

An hour later, Bernie didn't recognize herself in the mirror. The sage-green knit sweater was conservative, but soft and hugged her curves, the long sleeves ending in cuffs that made her wrists seem dainty.

The shoes wowed her the most. Strappy and showing off Bernie's one extravagance, a pedicure, they had a modest three-inch heel. Dana had tamed her copper curls just enough that they framed her face. And she'd talked Bernie into makeup. Not much, since Bernie didn't generally wear any, but sultry shadow, eyeliner, mascara, blush, and a touch of lip color.

"Just enough to make him want to kiss you, not enough to smear."

When Bernie turned this way and that, she couldn't believe how this small change had turned her from tomboy to...

"Sexy. A very sexy woman," Dana said.

"Wow. It's amazing."

"Holy shit!" Jen said from the doorway. "I almost didn't

recognize you."

"Thanks, kid. Good to know I'm an ugly witch most of the time. And watch the language."

"Yeah, yeah. I didn't mean you don't normally look fine and you know it. Dana, there are some folks in the store."

"Okay, I'll head out there. You critique."

Dana patted Bernie on the shoulder. "Don't let her tell you that you look anything but great. Beautiful. Ready for anything."

"Except walking in these heels," Bernie said, wobbling over to the bed and sitting down.

"Practice, practice, practice," Dana said with a wave.

"You think this will do?" Bernie asked Jen.

"I think Paul will be speechless. Your makeup is flawless. Do you think Dana would teach me how to do that?"

"Probably. When you're old enough."

"Ugh. Adults never think teenagers are old enough."

Bernie slipped the shoes off and put her flips on. "I should probably head back home soon. I need some time to practice walking before Paul picks me up."

"I found some cute journals in the shop," Jen said.

"I'll get them for you. We should think about paying you for your restaurant time anyhow."

"You've helped me so much, I want to repay the favor."

"No repayment needed, and at the very least, you deserve an allowance. You should have some spending money." Bernie looked her up and down. "And some new clothes. How about a shopping trip next day off?"

"That would be awesome!"

After Bernie paid for the journals, she and Dana watched Jen head for the beach with dog and puppy, laughing at their antics.

"She seems happy," Dana said.

"She's been cooped up in my apartment for close to two weeks. She's finally free. Well, sort of."

"The rest will work itself out. For now, happy is a good respite, eh?"

"Definitely." Bernie reached for the sweater and heels. "I can't thank you enough for the clothes."

"My pleasure. And Bernie? Enjoy tonight."

"It's been a while. A long while."

"Then enjoy it extra to make up for all that time. Relax. From what Josh says, Paul's good people. You deserve that. You deserve him. So just go with it."

"I'm going to try."

"Good. Now go home and finish getting ready. We'll see you tomorrow," Dana said, spearing Bernie with a look that said they'd better be talking tomorrow, too.

But, if all goes well, not every detail will be divulged. Just the thought of private details sent the butterflies skittering against the walls of Bernie's stomach again.

One moment at a time. One. Don't think ahead.

Chapter Thirteen

Paul was speechless. Absolutely unable to come up with a single word to describe the beautiful woman who stood before him. He was used to Bernie in no makeup, standard t-shirt and jeans, hair flying everywhere, or tightly bound in a ponytail.

This woman was someone completely different and he didn't know how to act.

Bernie walked up to him and gently closed his open mouth. "That, Mr. Gibson, is the best compliment you could have ever paid me." Her voice, low, sultry, and feminine, made things very uncomfortable inside his slacks. Paul relied on the method that had helped him on more occasions than he could count. He dissected, used rationality. Very little had changed about Bernie, yet everything had changed. Her hair was tamer, but not quite tamed. She wore makeup, but not a lot of it. The sweater showed no cleavage but branded her soft curves in all the right places. Her jeans... God save him, were they painted on?

And those heels. Paul had never considered himself to have a foot fetish, but he just might. Her legs went on forever.

"Oh, I almost forgot," Bernie said. "Let me get my phone."

She walked to the counter. Paul gulped as he watched her hips sway. He focused on the plan for the night. Dinner. They were having dinner. Not going to his condo. Dinner. Out. Except the plans he'd made were intimate, which meant he was in real trouble because he wanted to pull those clothes off slowly, one item at a time. Except for the shoes. Those would stay on until the last possible moment.

"You ready?" Bernie said, smiling at him.

"Are Josh and Dana here?"

"No. I took Bernie and Juniper to them. They're having movie night, and Juniper and Duffy are already old friends."

"Duffy?"

"Their dog."

As he watched Bernie head out the door and down the street, Paul had to yank his gaze away from her ass when he almost ran into a post. He raced ahead of her to open the door of his car. Just before he shut it, Bernie whispered.

"She's spending the night so there's no rush to get home."

Paul stumbled his way around the car, pulling at the loose collar of his Polo, taking a deep breath to calm himself before he got in. *Damn.* He was acting like a teenager in heat. Granted, it had been a while, but he'd done this before.

Except never with Bernie. And never with this level of emotion attached. His heart pounded and his palms were actually sweaty. Wiping them on his jeans, Paul looked up at the sky. "Lord, give me strength to be patient and show this woman in a thousand ways how much she's come to mean to me."

He got in the car, the light, airy fragrance of Bernie's perfume settling his nerves. Paul reached for Bernie's hand and brought it to his lips before settling it on his thigh. "Ready to have some fun?"

Even in the fading daylight, he could see her eyes darken with desire. "Yes," she said, barely breathing.

Good. It was nice to know he could affect her the way she affected him. Now all he had to do was get through dinner and pray she wanted to take things further.

~~~

Paul didn't head inland but instead drove up the coast. And not far, taking a left toward the beach. When the lighthouse came into view, Bernie looked at him, surprised.

Paul shrugged. "I thought we'd do something different from the norm."

When he parked, Bernie reached for her door handle.

"Don't you dare," Paul said, getting out and coming around the car to open the door.

This was so not Bernie. She took care of herself and didn't rely on anyone. Still, the small gesture nestled in her heart. For the first time in her life, she felt like a girl. Feminine. A woman. It was strange. Heady. Like smelling a fragrant rose, having the scent wrap around you like a gentle, heart-warming cocoon.

Did she like this feeling? Bernie nodded to herself as she took Paul's hand to exit the car. Yep. She could definitely get used to this.

Inside the lighthouse, her heart warmed even further. They walked through the gift shop and took the stairs up to the keeper's personal quarters. The small living area had a table for two set up, complete with candles, though they weren't lit at the moment.

"Intimate," Bernie said softly.

"Just what I'd hoped for."

"Do you know Luke?"

"The lighthouse keeper? It's funny how many people you can meet on the beach here. I was out for a walk and he was fishing, so we got to talking."

"He doesn't stay here full time."

"I know. He sleeps here when the weather is bad. Even though the lighthouse is automated, he likes to be here in case there are any issues."

"I'm surprised you got him to talk. He's a pretty quiet guy."

"Shy guys recognize each other. We have a club."

"You? Shy?"

Paul twirled one of Bernie's curls around his finger. "I worked to get over it."

Before she knew what she was doing, Bernie leaned toward him. He cupped her face in both hands. "You are so beautiful."

"It's the makeup."

"Stop it. No jokes tonight. It's not the makeup. I've fallen for you. Hard. And that was before tonight. Your eyes light up when people are around. They sparkle with a zest for life and crinkle at the corners when you laugh. They aren't so much green as they are a thousand different shades of green. Shades of life."

He kissed her with slow, tender care, proving every word he said with action and emotion.

"I noticed your body way before these skintight jeans." He cupped her butt and pulled her in tight.

Bernie's pulse quickened as she felt his need.

"The heels, though. Those really got my attention."

He kept kissing her in between sentences, and Bernie, dizzy with emotion and desire, clung to him for stability.

"They're borrowed."

"Then we might have to go on a shopping trip, because I'd like nothing better than to see you in heels... and nothing else."

"Oh," Bernie said, rather liking the idea of that.

"But first, dinner. And we've got a few minutes before it arrives. Want to go check out the top of the lighthouse?"

Still mired in the sensual air that cocooned them, Bernie murmured yes, not sure what she'd agreed to.

"Great." Paul backed up and Bernie almost slumped to the ground.

"Whoa, there. I've got you."

"Yes," she said, clearing her throat as the haze in her head dissipated. "You do."

Paul's eyes darkened and he backed up further. "View, dinner, then we explore. I promised myself we'd have a real date. You know... before."

"But the after sounds so much more fun."

"Don't toy with me. I planned this evening to the nth degree."

Bernie sighed and tamped down her libido, not an easy feat. He had done a lot of work for this night, and she owed it to him to enjoy it. Waiting wasn't going to be easy, but she'd do it. For him. "All right, then. Show me the view."

With a grin, Paul reached for her hand. They went up the stairs single file with him holding her hand behind his back. Once outside, the wind caught them and Bernie's carefully tamed hair turned wild. She didn't care. She was on top of the world.

"I've never been up here before," she said.

"Really? Then I'm glad we did this."

The pleasure in his voice warmed her from the inside out and she couldn't stop smiling. Paul leaned against the stucco wall and Bernie leaned against him, looking out over the water crashing into shore. Paul wrapped his arms around her and they stood there for several minutes, not speaking, just enjoying the moment and each other.

"I hear a car," he said. "That means dinner's here. Let's go eat."

Back inside, when Bernie saw the bags of food she couldn't believe it.

"That's my favorite restaurant, but it's forty minutes away from here. How did you manage this?"

"With Josh's help. He told me what restaurant and, it turns out, for the right price, they'll deliver. Sit and eat while it's hot."

Bernie felt the sting of tears and gulped to keep them at bay. No one had ever treated her with such consideration.

Ever. Between parents whose only thought was their next bottle to guys on the street who saw sex as a bartering tool, she'd never been… cared for like this. The swell in her heart almost overwhelmed her. She wanted to spend forever in this moment. Forever. She'd never thought in terms of that before. It was today, tomorrow, next week. Never longer than that in case she had to run.

Bernie shook the morbid thoughts out of her head and picked up her fork. Tonight was for enjoying, not reflecting.

Over a dinner of salads and chicken pesto, they talked a lot about Paul's life. He'd grown up with loving parents in a family of five kids. As the middle child, he'd often become the mediator, which had segued well into his job in social services.

"Do you still like the work?"

He looked around the small room, a frown on his face, which surprised Bernie.

"I thought this was a calling for you?" she said.

"It has been, until lately." He picked up her hand, absentmindedly toying with it. He was in a different world.

"I've always liked making sure kids are in the best possible situation and are well-cared for. That has been harder to accomplish lately. Parents put up smoke screens, kids lie. And nine times out of ten, regulations bind my hands so tight I can't help, at least not enough."

He drew imaginary lines in Bernie's palm.

"A few months ago, I lost a kid."

What? Lost? "As in missing?"

"As in dead. Killed by a dealer who worked for his father." Paul withdrew his hand and covered his face with it. "I shouldn't have sent him back to that house. I didn't want to, but there was no legal reason to stop it. Georgie pleaded with me not to send him back, but he never once gave away his father's secrets, whether out of loyalty or because of his father's threats, I don't know. But someone high up must have thought Georgie's father was a weak link and needed a reminder to keep those secrets close. His father found Georgie in his bed. Shot."

Paul lifted his head and tears glistened.

Awash in Paul's misery, Bernie came around the table and circled him with her arms. He clutched them, hung on to her.

"Since then, I've been trying to make amends. To make sure every kid has a chance at a good life. But it's meant knocking heads with my boss on a regular basis."

"Is Jen one of those head-knocking moments?"

Paul nodded and Bernie knelt before him, her hands on his knees. "I'm so sorry I dragged you into this."

"You didn't drag me. I want to help Jen. She may well be the last one I *can* help."

"What does that mean?"

"I've been thinking of re-directing my energy."

"Quitting?"

"Finding another way to help kids." Paul touched her cheek. "I didn't mean to bring all this up tonight. I wanted tonight to be about us. To be happy."

"It is about us. We're learning about each other, and this is an important part of you. I'm honored that you shared it with me."

"Something about you makes me want to open up. You have a way of making people feel comfortable, okay with baring their soul. My soul." He lifted her to his lap, cuddling her tight.

"I feel the same way."

He nuzzled her neck. "I don't want to talk about this anymore."

Bernie ran her hand through his short hair, leaning her head to give him better access. "I don't want to talk at all."

Paul pulled back. "Are we going to do this?"

"Do you have condoms?"

"I do." He smiled.

"Then I think we're going to do this." She returned his smile.

"Then let's clean this up, lock up, and go to my condo."

"The sooner, the better."

Within minutes, they were in Paul's car, Bernie's hand firmly in his as he navigated the road back to his condo. She gazed at him, leaning forward as if it would get them there faster. He glanced her way, a feral need darkening his blue eyes. She knew her own reflected that need. The vibration that thrummed through her caught Bernie off guard. No man had ever affected her this way and that scared her. Terrified her. Tonight, everything would change, not only between them, but deep in her soul, where she'd hidden all her yearnings to move beyond her past.

"You all right? You're pretty quiet." Paul asked.

Was she? Bernie wanted this. Wanted to be naked with Paul, to explore, to go beyond the physical and trust someone, something that had never worked out for her before. But this was different. Paul was different from anyone she'd ever met. Kind, caring, a good man. Yes, she wanted this. Him. More than anything.

Reaching up, she ran a hand through the curly hair at the back of his neck. "I'm okay."

"Still want— "

"Oh, yes. I definitely want." Bernie ran her hand along his arm, to his leg, and cupped him. "And so do you."

"Do I ever," he said, squirming.

Scant minutes later, they were climbing the stairs to his condo, stopping every third or fourth step for a heated kiss, giggling like teenagers.

"No elevator?"

"Nope. Good exercise. And more kissing time."

He pulled her into his arms.

"Third floor?"

"Best view."

He tugged her along the walkway, unlocked the door, then they were inside. Bernie caught a quick view of a tall table against the wall with Paul's laptop and paperwork strewn over it. Then the door closed with a soft chink and that was all she needed to turn into his arms and kiss him.

"I think I've wanted you since that first time you came to the restaurant," she said.

"I'm so glad I had a hankering for pizza that night."

They peeled coats off as they rounded the corner into the bedroom.

"Not the heels," Paul said.

"Can't get my jeans off wearing them."

"Good point. Let me, then."

Holy shit. Bernie had no idea how sexy being undressed by a man could be. Paul nudged her to the bed and knelt before her. He unstrapped one sandal and, with a sigh, set it aside. Then the other sandal, replacing it with his lips as he kissed first one foot, then the other.

"Foot fetish?" Bernie asked.

"Not until now. I'm a changed man because of you."

He rose and, kissing her with the promise of so much more, guided her to stand, running his hands down her arms until they settled on her hips. When they slipped under her sweater, Bernie shivered. Slowly, so slowly she wanted to rip the sweater over her head, he lifted the sweater.

"Taking your sweet time."

"Savoring the moment," he said, grinning. Paul then proceeded to unsnap her jeans, lowering the zipper one agonizing inch at a time. When he tugged to remove them, Bernie shuddered.

"Okay?"

"Better than okay."

She stepped out of the jeans and stood before him in the black bra and panties she'd never worn before tonight. Cool air didn't do one thing to stop the heat building within her as his eyes roamed her body. His gaze made her tingle until her entire body shook with need.

Bernie had never thought being ogled could be sexy. Until now. She had the feeling she was going to learn a lot of things tonight.

~~~

"You are so beautiful," Paul whispered. Almost too beautiful to touch. He'd never felt this strong an emotion, never wanted to undress a woman, be skin to skin, like he wanted to be with Bernie. If emotion added something this powerful to sex, he wanted more of it. A lifetime of it.

Bernie's hands had clenched. Paul reached for them, bringing one, then the other, to his lips.

"How come you're still dressed?" Bernie's voice, low and sultry, gave him tremors.

"I can take care of that."

"Please do," she said, laying down on the bed then raising her arms over her head in a languid stretch.

Paul shed his clothes in record time and joined her, almost afraid to touch her now that they were in bed. He lay there, staring at her, frozen until she wrapped her fingers around him.

"Crap," he yelped, throbbing under her hand. "Warn a guy, will you?"

"It's more fun this way." A slow, devilish smile followed.

"So it's going to be like that, is it?"

Bernie shrugged, sliding her fingers up and down his length.

Running his hand over her trembling stomach and up to the sheer lace bra, Paul encircled her breast, his thumb barely brushing over her nipple. Bernie gasped and let go of him, which gave him the advantage. He snapped the front hook, pushed the bra aside, and pulled her breast into his mouth, her writhing filling him with heady power and a desire to know every bit of her body. He loved her from breast to core, kissing, learning what made her gasp. What made her sigh with pleasure.

When she came the first time, he savored the moment, her taste, how happy it made him. He barely survived her sheathing him. Slipping inside her was the most intoxicating feeling of all. He'd come home. And he never wanted to leave again. He took things slow and easy, moving in and out, bringing her back to the brink until they crashed over the edge together in wave after wave of sensation.

Lying there, panting until reason righted their world, Paul found himself speechless. He'd never known the meaning of soul mate until now. God, if Bernie ever left him, he'd never survive. He'd given himself over to her.

Now all he had to do was find a way to tell her that without totally freaking her out.

Chapter Fourteen

Bernie drifted to wakefulness slowly, sublimely satisfied. She wanted to stay in this bed forever. She was comfortable here. Too comfortable. Where was the lump she always had to curl around to sleep? And why did these sheets feel so crisp and new?

Opening one eye, she looked around. Strange, generic pictures hung on the walls. Where was she?

Paul's condo. Bernie's eyes flew open as she turned her head to find his side of the bed empty. They'd rushed in last night, piling into bed like randy teenagers. No, actually, they hadn't. He'd peeled her clothes off in a partner-assisted strip tease that had been the sexiest thing ever. Sitting up, Bernie spied the heels on the floor. She'd definitely be buying some of those.

Lying back down, she stretched both arms out, then grabbed Paul's pillow and screamed her happiness into it.

"Do I hear screams?" Paul said as he entered with two cups. "Did you start without me?"

"Maybe. But I smell coffee. I'll gladly take a break for that." She sat up, bringing the sheet with her, and held out her hand.

"Is that joy for me or the coffee?"

Bernie took the cup and sniffed the heady scent appreciatively. "Right now, the coffee. But earlier, it was all for you."

"And it will be again." Paul set his cup down, then reached for hers.

Bernie tucked it into her chest. She really loved coffee. She needed coffee.

"I'll heat it up after. And I'll make it worth your while."

Oooh. He so knew how to do that. Bernie gave up her coffee without a fight as Paul tugged the sheet free and proceeded to show her exactly how worth her while it was.

~~~

Holy shit. Paul barely made it through a shower. He could barely stand. Not because he was exhausted. Because he was overwhelmed. Being with Bernie, making love with her, had rocked his world. Nothing had ever compared to this and Paul didn't think anything ever would.

He leaned against the shower wall, his heart beating so hard he rubbed his chest. As it hit him that he was head over heels in love with Bernadette Pedersen. He hadn't been looking for it. In fact, his life was so complicated he'd gone out of his way to keep entanglements at bay, not dating, not even putting himself in social situations. One visit to this oceanside town, one pizza and beer later, and he'd jumped right into the deep end.

"You about done in there?" Bernie said from the bedroom.

"Uh, yeah." Paul's voice cracked, so he tried again, stronger this time. "Just getting out." Bernie had showered first, citing the need for some privacy. Had she stood here utterly blown away, too? Had she struggled with the power of what had just happened?

God, he hoped so.

After drying off, he wrapped a towel around his waist and opened the door. Bernie was dressed and standing at the window, looking out at the ocean. She turned. The fire grew in her eyes as she gazed at him. She walked into his open arms and leaned against his chest.

"You make me forget everything," Bernie whispered.

"I can live with that," Paul said, breathing in her freshly shampooed hair. His soap, her scent. A heady mixture.

Bernie backed away with obvious reluctance. "I need to

open the restaurant. And pick up Jen and the puppy at Dana's shop. She's probably spent all of that money I gave her and cleaned Dana out of journals."

Paul chuckled and whipped off his towel. "I'll be dressed in a flash."

Her gaze dipped, but she looked up and sighed. "We don't have time."

"Not this morning," he said, his voice rough with longing. "But soon. Again."

"Yes, again."

A long moment passed before Bernie turned around. "Damn it. You'd better get dressed."

Paul chuckled and complied. A little while later, they walked into Tangerine Treasures.

"I'll get your sweater back to you soon," Bernie told Dana. "It's clean, but I'd like to have it dry-cleaned for you."

"No rush." Bernie must have noticed the obvious questions in her friend's eyes because she blushed the cutest shade of pink. Paul couldn't resist touching her. He encircled her from behind and rested his chin on her head. "Thanks, Dana. We appreciate you and Josh helping out."

"We enjoyed it. Jen's a gas to be around, and she earned her keep by doing the dishes and walking the dogs. Plus, Juniper and Duffy have become fast friends."

Jen joined them, the scruffy mutt in question and his new best friend at her heels. "He's adorable, Dana," Jen said. "I wish I could take Duffy home with me."

"You've already got a dog," Bernie said, laughing.

"And you can dog-sit any time you want."

"Awesome!"

After hugs all-around, Paul, Bernie, Jen, and Juniper headed back to Square Peg, sans Duffy. Paul loved how relaxed and happy Jen seemed, just like a teenager should be. He could see the same joy reflected in Bernie's eyes as she watched the girl.

"Let's head upstairs first," Bernie suggested. "I need to change, and we can do some food prep before your father arrives. I especially need out of these heels." She wobbled as she mentioned them, before she slipped them off to traipse up the stairs barefoot.

Jen and Paul chuckled and followed her. All three were laughing by the time Bernie opened the door.

"What the hell?"

All laughter died when they saw the inside of the apartment. Everything had been trashed. Tossed. Destroyed.

"Get out. Now. And call 911." Paul pushed Bernie and Jen behind him. "Whoever did this could still be here."

"Then let me at them," Bernie said with tears in her eyes.

She tried to push past Paul but he held her with everything he had. *Damn, this woman was strong.*

"Please, Bernie," he whispered in her ear. "I need you safe. I need Jen safe. Wait. I'm begging you."

Bernie stopped struggling and slumped against him for a moment, then pulled back. "All right. But don't try to pull that macho shit on me again, Gibson. Got it?"

He almost saluted as they all backed down the stairs. They didn't have to wait long before Jackson came roaring down the street, lights and siren going. He skidded to a halt in front of the restaurant and leaped out.

"The apartment's been trashed," Bernie said. With a look at Paul, she continued. "We don't know if someone's still in there."

"Is this the only way in and out?"

"Yes, unless you count the emergency ladder in my closet and the second-story window it fits."

"Okay. Wait here. I'm checking that window first."

A car skidded to a halt behind Jackson's cruiser and Josh leaped out, racing up. "Are you all okay?" He grabbed Bernie in a tight hug, then Jen, then, to Paul's surprise, him.

"We're fine," Bernie said. "Place is pretty trashed, though."

"What happened?"

Bernie put her hands on her hips. "Now, if we knew that, Mr. Morgan, we wouldn't be standing out here. We. Just. Got. Home."

"We called Jackson before we went in," Paul explained.

"Smart. I heard it on the scanner in my office."

They stopped talking when Jackson came down the stairs. "No one inside. They really did a number on the place, though. Sorry, Bernie."

Paul put his arm around her shoulder as tears filled her eyes. Suddenly, she clapped a hand over her mouth. "The restaurant."

They turned as one unit to the door.

"It still looks locked," Paul said.

"Wait here." Jackson re-pulled his weapon, walked over, and tried the door. "Seems locked. Bernie, keys?"

She dug them out and tossed them to him. He unlocked the door and disappeared inside. They all waited with bated breath until he came out.

"They didn't touch the restaurant as near as I can tell."

"Thank God, because I'd for sure kill them in that case."

"Probably shouldn't say that in front of the sheriff," Josh said, chuckling.

"Oh, there would be no doubt it was me who killed the bastards who did this. I'd carve my initials in their— "

"Bernie?" Paul said quietly.

She glanced at Jen. "Yeah, well, you know."

"Oh, yeah," Jen said, clutching Juniper's leash tight. "We all know."

"Can we go up?" Bernie asked.

"Yes. It's safe." Jackson patted her shoulder. "I'm sorry.

I'll drop off a report and form for you later that you can use for insurance."

"Thanks." Bernie's shoulders, previously straight with indignation, now slumped. Paul wanted nothing more than to take this pain away from her, but he couldn't.

"Want me to come up with you?" Josh asked.

Bernie shook her head. "Thanks, but Jen and Paul are here."

"Okay, but remember I'm only a phone call away." Josh hugged her, shook Paul's hand, and left. Jackson followed him down the road.

When Bernie, Paul, and Jen entered the apartment, what they found didn't even look like the result of a search. More like rage. Her couch was shredded, dishes flung against walls and broken. Something, hopefully ketchup, was splattered across the walls, counters, and floors. Book covers were torn off and her TV lay shattered in a thousand pieces on the floor.

They went down the hall to the bedrooms. Bernie's had been destroyed, much like the main area. By the smell of things, whoever did this had pissed all over her bedding and the mattress, which lay askew, spitting foam where a knife had slashed it open. The real surprise came when they opened Jen's door. Nothing was destroyed. The room was pristine, except for the fact that everything Jen owned was just... gone.

"What the hell?" Bernie said.

Jen raced in and pulled up the mattress. "They're gone." She dropped to the bed, her head in her hands. Sobs wracking her shoulders. Juniper leaped onto her, licking her hands until Paul pulled the pup away.

"What, baby?" Bernie said, sitting beside her and putting an arm around her shoulder.

"My journals," she cried. "All my thoughts. Agonies.

Everything. Oh, God, I can't stand that someone might be reading them. Right now. I bet that asshole Gavin did this."

Based on the heightened inflection in Jen's voice, she was close to hysteria. Paul stepped in front of her and squatted down. He pulling her into a hug. "I'm so sorry, Jen. So sorry." He rubbed her back over and over, murmuring words that meant nothing. The tone of his voice was the important part, proof that he felt her pain. He knew how to calm kids down. This was his forte.

But Jen was inconsolable. And, by the look on her face, so was Bernie. Filled with rage she couldn't vent.

"Why are these journals so important to you?" Paul asked gently.

"They're my proof. I wrote it all down. All my thoughts, worries, how I think M-Mom died."

Paul looked at Bernie's widening eyes. This wasn't good. And the fact that someone had singled out Jen's room meant they hadn't come for Bernie. Nope, not good at all.

"Hello? Uh, anybody home?"

Oh, shit. They'd planned their arrival at home to give them some time with Jen before her bio-dad showed up.

"I c-can't," Jen squeaked. "Not right now. I just can't."

"It's okay," Bernie said, cocking her head, indicating that Paul should stay with Jen.

He didn't like it, but it was the better choice for Jen's sake.

"I'll take care of this," Bernie said, walking out.

Chapter Fifteen

Bernie's heart broke as she watched Jen's frantic eyes dart around the room. She knew that look. *Find a place to hide.*

"Don't worry. I'll reschedule." She left the bedroom, stepping over and around debris to reach the main room. The burglar had apparently left the front door wide open because a nice-looking couple stood there, the woman standing a bit behind the man, his arm protecting her.

"Is everything all right?" he asked.

"No. I'm sorry. We got broken into, probably just over the last couple of hours," Bernie said, waving her hand to indicate the room. "This is all damage."

"Wow. Whoever did this really went to town." The man glanced around again, then at Bernie. His eyes were the same brilliant blue as Jen's. There was no doubt in Bernie's mind this was bio-dad. When he thrust out his hand, she shook it.

"I'm Michael Robbins." He dropped his hand and his wife moved beside him. She pushed thick brown curls out of her eyes. "This is my wife, Andrea. Paul Gibson gave us this address."

Bernie tried to smile but all she could think about was that these people could take Jen from her. The kid had become important. Losing her was going to hurt. "I'm Bernie, and this is the right address. I know we set this time to meet, but this has thrown us all for a loop."

"We've reserved a place here for a couple days. I'll admit, I'm anxious to meet my—Jen—but I'm guessing everyone's pretty emotional right now."

"We are."

"Would tonight work better?"

"Umm, it would, if it could be after the restaurant

closes. Say, nine p.m.? Is that too late?"

He shook his head emphatically. "Anytime will be fine. All right, we'll leave you to... this... and see you at nine tonight."

"Thanks. Just come in through the restaurant doors. We'll be there."

"Good. As you can imagine, we're excited to meet her, but we can wait a few more hours."

After they left, Bernie gave herself a stern talking-to. They both looked so excited, so hopeful, she couldn't dislike them. But damn it, she didn't want to lose Jen, either. Shaking her head, she went back to the bedroom, where Paul and Jen sat with their heads together, murmuring between them.

"Are they gone?" Jen asked, raising her head.

"Until tonight. They'll meet us in the restaurant after it closes."

"Are they— What do they— "

"They look nice. He's handsome and you have his eyes." Bernie smiled, even though she didn't feel like it. "They are very excited to meet you."

Paul stood and hugged Bernie. She didn't know how, but he must know what she was thinking. She hugged him back.

"The restaurant opens in an hour and we've got some things to do before then," Bernie said, holding up the heels that still dangled from her hand. "I'm going to change, then we can spend half an hour cleaning up, then half an hour prepping in the restaurant."

"You're not staying here tonight. My condo has a fold-out couch. You can both sleep at my place."

Bernie would have argued with him making choices for her, but she didn't have the energy. She nodded. "Okay, let's pack bags."

Jen started to cry again. Bernie looked at Paul.

"There's nothing left of her stuff here," he said. "Not one damn thing."

"Shoot. Okay." She went and sat on the bed by Jen. "How about you and Paul go shop for some essentials for you. A couple new outfits, shoes, bathroom stuff. I'll get the restaurant open and you can join me later." Maybe a shopping spree would divert Jen's worries, at least for a while.

"I'm game if you are," Paul said.

"Are you sure you don't need my help?" Jen asked, though her face had already lightened. The idea of new clothes helped.

"I've run this place solo for a lot of years. I think I can handle one more day. Besides, Juniper will help." She tried to smile but it died quickly. "It won't be as fun without you here, though."

Jen hugged her and Juniper. A few minutes later Bernie closed the door behind them and turned and surveyed the mess, already missing them both. Funny, she'd been a loner her entire life and had never needed anyone. Now, both Jen and Paul had filled gaping holes in her heart she hadn't even known were there.

Sliding down the front door to sit on the floor with an arm around the puppy, Bernie gave into the melancholy, something she rarely allowed. Everything in her life was changing, some things for the good and some, not so much. Bernie had spent so many years not knowing what tomorrow would bring that once she'd settled, she'd maintained a normal, predictable life. That had always worked for her and kept the memories at bay. Now, emotions she'd taught herself to hide lay flayed out on her sleeve for everyone to see. And Paul saw more than most.

Not completely sure she liked these changes in her

world, she sighed and hauled herself up to go change into jeans and a t-shirt. Miraculously, her clothes hadn't been touched, even though she'd never put them away. She closed the apartment door behind her, trying to push the break-in out of her mind. She went downstairs, put Juniper in the kennel she kept next to the storeroom, and started to prep for her workday. She needed the familiar around her. The scent of pizza sauce, the feel of kneading dough. Normal.

~~~

Through his years of helping children, mostly teens, with their home situations, Paul Gibson could honestly say he'd never been shopping with a teenage girl. What an experience! They'd driven to the closest mall, a little less than an hour away, and Jen had pulled him into every store in the place, just about. All concern about her journals had disappeared while they were there. Two hours later, armed with bags holding new jeans, shirts, shoes, and various other teenage "survival" items, like makeup and a new journal, they drove back to Willow Bay. Jen wore new clothes, including a bedazzled jean jacket. He'd made her get a warmer coat, citing unpredictable ocean weather, but couldn't resist the look in her eyes when she'd clutched this jacket to her. His credit card bill would be bulging this month.

Worth it.

"You've gotten pretty quiet," he mentioned after a few minutes on the road.

"Yeah. Just processing."

"I get it. It was a rough morning."

She'd been so happy the last day or so, then for this to happen? What a rollercoaster of emotions.

Out of the corner of his eye, he caught her nod.

"You worried about meeting your biological father tonight?"

At first, he didn't think she'd answer him. When she did,

it all came out in a rush.

"I'm worried he'll take me away. I want to stay here. With Bernie. With you. I don't want to leave. I don't want to like him. If he wants me to live with him, I'll have to move to Portland and I'll never see you again."

There it was, buried in the center of her dialogue. *I don't want to like him.* That was probably what worried her most. Paul had seen it before. She had a stable situation and didn't want to rock the boat. Didn't want to want to do that. Loyalty was everything when you lived on the street. It's what kept you safe. Loyalty to yourself in the beginning, then loyalty to your gang. The people you banded with.

"Whether you like him or not, in my official capacity, no decision will be made tonight. This is just a meet and greet. That's all. Does that help?"

When the air whooshed out of her lungs, he almost laughed.

"Yeah. It does. A lot." Jen reached down to the bags she wouldn't let him put in back and started pulling things out and looking at them.

Paul chuckled. Teenage focus changed quickly.

Back in town, Paul dropped Jen off with all her bags and told her to tell Bernie he'd see her later. He planned to eat dinner at Square Peg, then stick around until after the meeting when they'd all head back to his place.

He'd barely gotten inside the door to his condo when his phone rang. His boss. Well, no time like the present. He punched the green button.

"Your ass is fired."

"I figured."

"I'm sending someone to pick up the girl tomorrow. Have her ready." He hung up without waiting for Paul's answer.

Damn. Everything was piling up. He didn't mind about

the job. This had been a long time coming and it was time for a change. He thought about his new credit-card burden. Still worth it. He'd just have to find a way to pay it off.

Right now, Jen was the bigger issue. Everything in her life was converging. Paul parked at his condo and went inside, praying things went well tonight. And that whoever they sent from the office tomorrow would work with the situation, not destroy it. If it was Georgia, she'd listen. Greta or John would take a hard line.

Either way, tomorrow was going to be decisive. Jen was smack dab in the middle of a tug-of-war. Paul knuckled his closed eyes, feeling the beginnings of a headache and praying things sorted themselves out so everyone was happy.

He moved to the patio and stared out at the waves. Just once, could everything turn out all right? Please?

Chapter Sixteen

Bernie wiped her hands on her red apron one more time. She never sweat this much, except when there was a lot at stake. The last time, she'd been hunkered down behind a trash bin in the middle of the night, just trying to get a little sleep. A drug deal gone wrong right in front of her eliminated that possibility. She'd breathed as quietly as possible, not moving, afraid to make any noise as the junkie got the crap beat out of him.

Shaking her head to dispel long-buried memories, Bernie reminded herself this wasn't life or death. Only a meeting. Either way, Jen would be okay. In fact, Bernie was probably the only one who'd lose out. She'd grown too fond of Jen and loved having her around.

Bernie watched as Jen grabbed a dirty dish tote and headed out into the restaurant, reminding herself that this wasn't about her. This was about getting Jen into the best possible situation, so she'd thrive and grow into all the possibilities in front of her. That should be Bernie's focus.

So why did her heart feel like it was breaking?

"It's going to be all right," Paul said, wrapping his arms around her. The restaurant was almost empty. Only one more table finishing up, then they'd be and ready for the meeting. Bernie clutched Paul's arms. Would she ever be ready?

"You know, I really hate that I like the guy already."

He smiled against her neck. "I know."

"I want what's best for Jen." Did she? Or did she selfishly want to keep the girl here at all costs?

"You do."

"So why am I so nervous?" Bernie rubbed her hands on

her apron again.

Paul turned her around, his serious face on. "Because you care."

"Is it this hard for you when you have to let kids go?"

"Sometimes. I always worry." He hesitated for a moment, then hugged her. "Everything's going to work out fine. I feel good about this, sweetheart. But no decisions tonight. This is just to meet each other. Remember that."

Bernie nodded as she saw the last customers rise from their table and head for the counter to pay. She touched Paul's cheek. "Thank you."

"Anytime." His eyes crinkled at the corners as he smiled. Just for a moment, she got lost in them.

Disentangling herself, Bernie took care of the customers while Jen and Paul bussed the table. The bell jangled as they left and Jen froze. *Damn. Poor kid's a basket case.*

Just like Bernie herself was. *Run!* The fleeting thought raced through her mind, but the bell jangled again. Too late.

Bio-dad and his wife walked in, nervous expectation written all over their faces. And Jen stood in the middle of the restaurant with a tray full of dirty dishes in her hands.

Bernie took a deep breath. It was suck-it-up time, so while Paul took the tray from Jen, Bernie introduced them. "Jen, this is Michael and Andrea. And this—" she put her arm around Jen's shoulders, tightening it briefly—"is Jen."

No one rushed to hug anyone, which Bernie gave the Robbins' credit for. Instead, Michael extended his hand. "It's so nice to meet you, Jen."

Jen stared at the hand, then slowly extended hers. Michael kept the touch brief and dropped his hand, and Bernie had to respect that. The man had good instincts.

Paul joined them and introduced himself. "Why don't we all sit down so we can chat."

Bernie and Jen sat on one side, Michael and Andrea on

the other. Paul let Juniper out of her kennel, figuring she'd help Jen deal. Then he pulled up a chair and sat at the end of the table like a moderator, smiling at everyone.

"You have your father's eyes," Andrea said.

"They're my eyes. Not his. He wasn't around."

Oh, this was going soooo well. Bernie itched to get involved, but she waited. There were things to talk about, to get out in the open, and it wasn't her place to censor Jen's words.

"I wasn't," Michael said, dipping his head for a moment. When he raised it, Bernie could swear she saw a sheen of tears in his eyes. "If I'd known, I'd have been there."

On the street, you learned to require proof before you accepted anything as truth. There wasn't any way Michael's statement could be proven.

"How did you and Mom meet?"

Michael clutched Andrea's hands in his. "I'm going to preface this story by saying I was a different man back then. I was in the army, buzzing through town on leave and full of oats and vinegar. I'm a long-haul trucker now."

"I know. Do you have a woman in every town?"

He squinted for a moment. "I had a few, but I knew your mother before all that."

Bernie glanced at Andrea. She knew this story and wasn't surprised. That respect meter inched up another notch.

"I have always remembered your mother. She was beautiful and full of a zest for life unlike anyone else I'd known, until Andrea."

Jen's eyes widened. "Most of what I remember is her being beaten down and depressed."

"I'm sorry to hear that. I'm also very sorry to hear she's gone. I can't even imagine your pain." He started to reach across the table, but Jen pulled her hands down onto her lap, so he stopped. That didn't faze Michael. He kept going.

"When my leave was over and I shipped out, we wrote back and forth. I was mesmerized by her and those feelings only grew while I was overseas. I'd planned to ask her to marry me when I got back. I only had a few months left in the service." He took a deep breath. "Then she stopped sending me letters."

Wait. What? Bernie glanced at Paul and Jen. Judging by their saucer eyes, they were stunned, too.

Michael pulled a small box out of his pocket. "When I got home, I rolled into Redding with this." He opened it to show a small diamond ring.

"Wait. Redding? California?" Jen asked. "That can't be my mom. We lived in Vancouver."

"When I got to her apartment in Redding, she was gone. Moved out. I convinced the manager to open the place for me. I refused to believe she'd left me until I saw it with my own eyes. The place was empty, except for one thing. The other half of this." He held out a chain with half of a heart on it.

Jen stared at the necklace for so long that everyone started to squirm.

With tender reverence, Jen reached down the neckline of her t-shirt and pulled out a chain with the other half of the heart hanging from the end of it.

They all stared at it. Proof positive, and better than any DNA test. Bernie tried to hide the tears that threatened. She was beyond grateful to be part of this special moment, as Jen stared at her father. The bittersweet knife dug in a little deeper before Bernie could stop it.

"It's the only thing I kept of Mom's. She wore it always. When she died, I wore it." Jen fingered the jagged piece of heart. "Why would she do that? Just leave and not tell you, then wear this reminder all those years?"

"I don't know." Michael shrugged. "Now, I think she

might have been pregnant with you at the time."

"But why leave?"

"I'm as confused about that as you are. She had my home address but never sent me another letter, never let me know where she'd moved to. No phone calls. Not even a text. I called her phone, but the number had been disconnected. I had no idea why she'd left or where she'd gone."

"If you're hoping I have answers, I don't. I never even knew she lived in California."

"I guess that's a mystery we'll both have to learn to live with. The year after that was pretty rough on me. I stopped every time I rolled through Redding, just on the off chance that she'd moved back. Eventually, I changed my route to a northern one so I wouldn't have to go anywhere near Redding. On one of my diner stops outside of Portland, I met Andrea."

She smiled. "I waitressed at the DoubleBar. He was seated in my section and we got to talking in between customers."

"From then on, every time I came into town, I stopped."

"And sat in my section."

"We've been married for ten years now." Michael looked at Andrea and even Bernie could see the love glowing between them. When he turned back, he put his hands together and placed them on the table, obviously torn about something.

"We can't have kids," Andrea said in a rush. "Something in my body rejects them."

"But we've always wanted them," Michael said. "Which is why we were both so excited to learn about you, Jen. We don't want to rush you or ask you to do anything you don't want to do, but we'd like to be part of your life in any way you'd allow us to."

Jen's hand reached over and clutched Bernie's. "I'm happy here."

"Good. I'm glad you are," Michael said. "Can I ask what brought you here? You lived in Vancouver."

Jen looked at Bernie, who nodded. They deserved to know.

"Vancouver was the only place I ever lived. It was Mom's house, but her boyfriend, Gavin, took it over like it was his. I can't stand him. He has a mean streak."

Michael stiffened. "Did he hit you?"

"Me? Only once. But Mom... "

Her words drifted off. There was no need to finish the sentence.

"After Mom died, I ran away." She glanced at Paul. "When social services found me, they sent me back to live with Gavin. So I ran away again, and this time I got out of Vancouver. I hitched a ride here. An old lady found me and pulled me into this restaurant. Bernie saved me. Got me off the streets and gave me a home. I feel safe here." She glanced upstairs. "Felt safe."

Michael looked at Bernie. "The break-in?"

She nodded. "We still have no idea why, though there's a clue. The place was trashed, all except Jen's room. And everything she owned was gone."

"Do you think this is related to Jen?"

"Seems like it." Bernie shrugged. "We're concerned it might have been Gavin. Jen hasn't been around Willow Bay long enough to tick anyone else off." She smiled, making sure the kid knew it was a joke.

"Are you safe?" Michael asked Jen.

"Bernie and Paul keep me safe."

Michael raised an eyebrow and glanced at Paul. "Getting personally involved?"

"Way beyond that. To be honest, I'm no longer a social worker with Vancouver CPS."

"What?" Bernie said. This was news to her. She watched Paul closely to see how he felt about it.

"I was supposed to take Jen back yesterday, hand her over to Gavin, and show up at the office today to work on my other cases, off this one from here on out. That didn't sit right with me. Why not keep Jen in a stable situation, that she likes, while this all gets figured out? People are made emergency foster parents all the time. We just hadn't gotten to that yet. And now, it's out of my hands." Paul looked at Bernie. "My ex-boss called me just before I got here. He's sending someone to pick Jen up tomorrow, and I've been fired."

"No!" Jen said, leaping up. "I'm not going back there."

Paul reached a hand out to her and, hesitantly, she took it. She sat back down.

"You're not going back there." Bernie listened in horror once again as Paul laid out the whole story about Gavin's sketchy past for Michael and Andrea. "After the response I got from my boss yesterday, I decided to turn over the evidence I have about him to a friend on the police force. He said he'd check it out, but that was only this morning."

Tears filled Michael's eyes. "I'm so sorry, Jen. So sorry we didn't know. About you. About the situation. Sorry you had to go through any of this."

Confusion filled Jen's face. Bernie could guess what she was feeling. She didn't want to like her bio-Dad. It was more than evident. That she seemed to like him despite her intentions was a good sign. For her, at least. Bernie clutched her own hands beneath the table as she saw Jen slowly slipping away from her. She couldn't stop the tide from coming in, and wouldn't. But damn, it hurt to think of losing her.

The sympathy she saw in Paul's eyes about undid her. Fighting back tears, she got back in the game.

"So, tonight is just an introduction."

Both Michael and Andrea nodded. "Can I hold your hand, Jen?" he asked.

Reluctantly, she held it out. Michael stared at her small hand encompassed in his larger one.

"I'm so happy to meet you. As I mentioned, Andrea and I want to be part of your life in any way we can. No pressure."

"How can you say that after one short meeting?"

Michael and Andrea glanced at each other, but Andrea spoke. "We consider ourselves pretty good judges of character. Michael said your mom was good people, so she'd have raised you with good values. Your life with her just got cut short way too soon. Plus, well, look at how quickly these two have come to care about you." She gestured at Bernie and Paul. "That in itself is a huge testament to the kind of person you are."

"We would take you home with us tonight if we could," Michael added. "We want you to live with us, to be our daughter in every sense." He held up his hand at Jen's wide eyes. "Don't worry. We know that's a big decision, and we don't want you making the choice rashly. We're willing to take the time for us all to get to know each other better. And if, in the end, you decide we aren't a good fit, we'd like to find a way to still be part of your life. Somehow. You are in the driver's seat, Jen. We won't force you, but we do hope you come to like us, at least a little."

Jen hung her head and Bernie saw tears dampening her new jeans. Juniper laid her head in Jen's lap.

"You all need time to think about this," Michael said. He and Andrea stood. "We'll go back to our hotel. Jen, would you be willing to have breakfast with us? We can pick you up, go to that restaurant by our hotel, and bring you back afterward."

Everyone waited, barely breathing, until Jen nodded her head, her hair still covering her lowered face.

Michael smiled. "Okay then. We'll pick you up at ten."

After they left, Paul locked the restaurant door and Jen finally lifted her head.

"What do you think of them?" he asked.

"I like them." She almost spit out the words.

Bernie laughed. "You don't have to sound so pissed about that."

"Yes, I do. I don't want to like them. I don't want to leave here, go live in some middle-class community with a white picket fence, go to school."

"You don't want to go to school?" That was quite different from how voraciously Jen devoured the school resources Bernie had found online for her.

"Well, maybe that. But I can do that here." Suddenly, she hugged Bernie tight. "I don't want to leave you. I like it here."

Bernie's heart swelled. "We're not making any decisions tonight, but I have to say, so far, I like Michael and Andrea. As much as I'd love to have you stay, they can probably give you more stability."

Jen slapped her hand on the table. "Bullshit."

"Jen!" Paul barked.

"Sorry, but I could be just as happy here as there."

"And I applaud you for considering both options," Bernie said. "For tonight, though, why don't you go pack what you need of those new clothes Paul bought you. We'll take Juniper over to Josh and Dana's and head to Paul's. Tomorrow, we'll come back here by ten. You can go to breakfast and I'll get some cleaning done upstairs."

"I want to help," Jen said.

"And you will. Trust me, I can't clean up that mess in an hour."

"'Kay." Jen headed to the kitchen where she'd left her purchases.

Bernie and Paul both stood. Bernie walked into his open arms.

"She's going to be okay either way, isn't she?" Bernie said.

"I think so."

"If she leaves, it's going to hurt like hell."

"I've gotten pretty attached to her myself. This isn't going to be easy. And someone from CPS is showing up tomorrow to take her away. We have to figure out how to handle that."

Paul kissed her and Bernie lost herself in the feel of him, warm, comforting, loving. She let out a long sigh and he laughed.

"I think we all need to decompress and figure out tomorrow when it gets here," Bernie said.

"Can't decompress the way I'd like to with a teenager sleeping on the couch."

A commotion in the kitchen got their attention. Pans hitting the floor, a muffled... scream?

Paul raced around the counter, Bernie on his heels. The back door was wide open and no one was in the kitchen. Not Jen, not anyone. Bernie's heart hit her throat. They raced outside in time to see red taillights speeding away down the street.

"Jen!" Bernie screamed. Over and over, she called her name while Paul dialed 9-1-1.

~~~

Paul stuck to Bernie's side, continually re-wrapping the blanket around her shoulders as she paced. It was all he could do, but nothing reduced his own frantic worry. Jen had been kidnapped and it had to be Gavin. What the hell was so important about Jen that he'd resort to this action? It had to be monetary, but he couldn't possibly think kidnapping her would help him get at her mother's money.

After Jackson had ordered roadblocks, street searches, and taken their statement, Paul finally thought to call Michael and Andrea, who were on their way over.

"They have a stake in this," he'd said to Bernie, and she'd nodded, throwing off the blanket once again.

"God, I can't stand this. I need to be out there searching, doing something."

"What can you do? Where can you search? Jackson is out there. Hell, I even called my ex-boss and let him know. The social worker he reassigned to Jen's case is on her way. Jackson's asked Vancouver police to check on Gavin, and there's an ABP out for his car."

"But we're not sure it's him. Jen never told me much about her time on the streets. What if it's some druggie or pimp she pissed off?"

To stop Bernie from pacing, Paul pulled her around so he could see her face. "What was your time like that you would even think of that?"

Bernie wouldn't look at him. "Bad, but that's neither here nor there. Right now, we need to focus on finding Jen."

"Agreed," he said, letting her go. "But one of these days, we're going to have a long talk."

"Maybe. Maybe not."

Michael and Andrea rushed in the door. "Any word?" Paul shook his head.

"Is there anything we can do?"

"Just wait," Bernie said. "Just sit and fucking wait." She glanced at the trio in front of her. "Sorry. I swear when I'm anxious."

"I can understand that," Michael said. "Trust me. I

know some you've probably never heard."

Bernie shook her head. "I doubt that."

The change in topic seemed to help everyone relax until Jackson walked through the door. "Wanted to give you an update," he said, "though there's not much to tell."

"Yes?" they all said in unison.

Jackson looked at Michael and Andrea.

"Jen's bio-dad, er, biological father and his wife. They are just as invested in getting her home safely as we are," Bernie said.

Jackson nodded. "Okay. We think you're on the right track and that her kidnapping is related to the ex. You know Willow Bay. We notice the abnormal."

"It's a good thing, too," Bernie said, nodding.

"Well, Gladys," Jackson continued with a glance at Michael and Andrea, "our local street person, was on her way home and noticed an unusual car parked across the street from here. There were a couple guys inside, but she couldn't see who in the dark. However, being the intrepid person she is, she wrote down the license plate." Jackson pulled a crinkled piece of paper out of his pocket. "It's Gavin's car."

"Shit," Bernie said.

"So what's that mean?" Michael said. Andrea clutched his hands.

"It means we can zero in on a specific search. Police have checked his address in Vancouver. Dark, and no one is home. No one near the entrances to town has seen his car, so we're hopeful we got the net up fast enough and he's still here."

"Then we need to find him." Bernie planted herself in front of Jackson. "How do we find him?"

Jackson took a deep breath. "*We* don't do anything. *You* stay right here. *I've* got the search going already."

"How?" Paul asked, pulling Bernie the Bulldog off

Jackson. "I hear this is a one-sheriff town."

"Maybe, but I've got a lot of friends. There are at least ten officers here right now, searching every nook and cranny of Willow Bay and asking questions. The state patrol has an eye on the highways." Jackson looked at Michael and Andrea, then back at Bernie. "If she's here, we'll find her."

And if she's not? God, Paul had been there too many times. A child disappears and eventually, no one remembers to keep looking.

"I can help," Paul said.

"No, you can't."

Everyone turned to the doorway to find a tall, thin, black woman with stylish hair, in paint-splotched clothes. "Sorry I'm late. Didn't even stop to change. We were painting."

"Georgia!" Paul said, stepping close to hug her.

"Don't you Georgia me, Paul Gibson. You're in a world of trouble."

"I know, but that's not the problem at the moment."

"So I've heard. Introduce me so I know the players."

"Everyone," Paul said, keeping his arm around his coworker's shoulder, "this is Georgia. She's a social worker from my office."

"Ex-office, you mean."

Chagrined, Paul nodded.

"All right. Sheriff Jackson, I heard most of your report," Georgia said. "Any more to add?"

"Not at this time."

"Then scoot. Get out there and find our girl."

"Yes, Ma'am!" Jackson said, pulling his hat on and winking at Paul as he headed for the door. Paul grabbed his coat to follow.

"Oh, no you don't, Mr. Gibson. You let the authorities take care of this. You're like one of the parents now, not here in an official capacity anymore. Besides"—Georgia glared at Paul—"You've got some explaining to do."

~~~

While Paul hunkered down at one table with the formidable Georgia, Bernie, Andrea, and Michael sat at another one as far away as possible. She didn't envy Paul the grilling he was about to endure. "Maybe I should go back him up."

"I think Paul can hold his own. He might not like the interference," Josh said, having arrived with Dana and Duffy shortly after Georgia. Juniper and Duffy lay together in the corner, watching the goings-on with soulful eyes.

"Do you know anything more?" Michael asked him.

Josh shook his head. "I wish I did. I was organizing search groups while Jackson updated you. As soon as he got back, I came here."

Bernie started when Michael slapped his hand on the table. "This is so frustrating. I didn't come here to meet my teenage daughter for the first time, only to have her stolen from me." He stood and paced for a minute, then sat back down. "Look," he said to Bernie, "I know this isn't your fault, but the situation happened. As soon as they find Jen, I'm taking her where she'll be safe. We're taking her home with us."

Bernie half stood as she planted her palms on the table. "You can't do that."

"I'm her father."

"Biologically only."

"That's more than you are."

"I'm the first person who helped her when she was in dire need."

"And look where she is now. Right back in the middle of that dire need."

How dare he? Bernie's hands curled into fists. Before

she could take action, Josh pulled her back into her chair. "Nobody is taking anybody anywhere. When we find Jen, we'll sort this out. Legally."

"Yes, we will," Georgia said, as she and Paul joined them.

Bernie got up to pace. "I don't do sit-and-wait well. I need some action. I'm going upstairs to clean."

Paul stood but she waved him off. "Please. I just need to be alone for a bit."

Paul frowned and the creases on his forehead grew even deeper, but he sat. Just for a moment, gratitude dulled the abject fear that coursed through Bernie's body. How had she managed to find someone so wonderful? She kissed him. "Thank you."

He nodded, still grim-faced. Bernie blocked it out and headed upstairs to her destroyed apartment. Standing in the middle of the mess, she couldn't decide where to start. A sob escaped and she squatted down, hands over her face, and let herself cry.

Once the dam broke, the tears wouldn't stop. It was several long minutes before Bernie took great, gulps of air to calm herself. Why was all this happening? And why Jen? The kid was goodness personified and didn't deserve this, damn it.

Bernie kicked at a shredded couch cushion. Standing here doing nothing was eating her up. She needed action. And, damn it, she was going to take action. Heading to her bedroom, she found the switchblade she hadn't touched since she'd moved in. She stuck it in her back jeans pocket and grabbed a jacket. As Bernie crept down the stairs with hard-learned stealth, she glanced in the restaurant window. The thought that she was about to give Paul a world of additional worry stopped her for a moment.

But Jen needed her, and hopefully, Paul would

understand. Skirting the back side of the restaurant, Bernie headed off down the street at a jog. She had an idea she wanted to check out. Only one place in town was big enough to hide a car and three people.

She reached the old cannery in fifteen minutes. Slated to be torn down next week and turned into a park, the cannery had been abandoned for years. Crumbling walls and gaping holes told of the ravages of seaside weather and disuse, but the part near the double doors in the back was protected and in pretty good shape.

Utilizing all the skills she'd learned during her days and nights on the street, Bernie crept close to those double doors. They were closed, but the moonlight revealed the circular arc on the ground of a recently opened door. Peeking in through the slats, she saw the car. She heard voices, though muffled. She tugged on the door and it gave, quietly, just enough for Bernie to slip inside. Using the darkness as cover, Bernie edged around the car until she saw them.

"I won't," Jen screamed, her voice loaded with stubborn.

"You'll come back with me and sign over your mother's assets or you'll learn the true meaning of pain, little girl," said one man, presumably Gavin, based on Paul's description.

Bernie reached for her phone. She didn't have Jackson's number, so she texted Paul.

Old cannery. Send Jackson.

"Yeah," the other man said, grabbing Jen's face and turning her to look at him. "Pain. And then some."

"As soon as this damn town stops searching for you, we're heading back to take care of things, all nice and legal."

"I'll tell anyone around us that you've kidnapped me."

"Who's going to believe a runaway? Besides, I've got legal guardianship."

Jen ripped her chin from the other man's hand and

glared at Gavin. "You won't get out of Willow Bay because they won't stop looking for me. You are going down, asshole. Big time."

Bernie jumped at the resounding slap that made Jen stumble. When Jen caught her balance, she spit, hitting Gavin square in the face. He pulled his hand back to hit her again, but never got the chance.

Bernie leaped forward and grabbed his arm, spinning him around. She clocked him with a right hook and followed up with a kick squarely between the legs. He slumped to the ground, moaning, as the other man leaped toward her.

"Don't even think about it," a voice said from behind her.

Jackson! Thank God.

The man froze, putting his hands up. When Bernie glanced behind her, Jackson stood there, gun drawn. Two deputies stood with him. And Paul. With things under control, Bernie raced to Jen, whose arms were tied.

"Oh, God, I'm so glad you're okay," Bernie said, alternately hugging her and leaning back to check her over. "We've been worried sick. Thank God." Over and over again, Bernie mumbled and hugged.

"I'm okay, I swear." Jen's muffled voice came from against Bernie's chest. "Though I'd really like it if someone could untie me."

"Got it," Paul said, glaring at Bernie while he cut the rope. Then he pulled both of them into his arms. "I've never been so scared in my life as I was tonight. Don't ever, ever do that to me again."

"Umm,"—again, Jen's voice was muffled—"Not like I had a choice."

"I'm not talking about you."

"He's talking to me," Bernie said as they parted. "I kind of snuck out to come find you."

"Kind of snuck out?" Paul said. "When I realized you were gone, the floor dropped out of my world."

"I had a hunch and needed action, so I followed it," Bernie said.

"You put yourself in danger when you could have let Jackson handle it."

"Jackson did handle it. I texted you and he came. And you need to know that I'd do it again, to keep Jen safe." She leaned toward Paul as she said it, pointing a finger at his chest.

Jen, who'd moved a safe distance away, stood with Jackson. The other deputies had taken Gavin and his accomplice off to jail.

"You think we should stop this?" Jen said. "Break them apart?"

Jackson grinned. "Nah. They'll work it out. Come on, kid. I'll take you back to the restaurant."

"But what about them?"

"Let them walk. It'll cool them off."

Though Bernie heard them, it didn't register as she and Paul went head-to-head.

"You can't go off half-cocked like that Bernie."

"I protect what's important to me."

Paul ran both hands through his hair. "So this is what comes of your street time? You're a scrapper who skirts the law and stares danger in the face? Is that a thing for you? Do you get off on danger?"

"No. And you know that's not me."

"I thought I did, but for you to go off like that on your own and never even give me a chance to help— "

"You would've tried to talk me out of it." She stuck her hands on her hips. "Tried to stop me."

"Hell, yes, I would have. What you did was stupid." Paul grabbed her arms and shook her. "You could have died."

Bernie crumbled at the anguish in his voice. She sank to the dirt floor, boneless beneath the worry she'd caused him. "I'm sorry, Paul. I'm so sorry I cause you so much worry. I wasn't thinking about that. Only about getting to Jen."

Paul sat down beside her, his hair wild from being raked so many times. He reached for her hand and cupped it in both of his and they sat there for a while, breathing. Thinking.

"Maybe you haven't completely left your other life behind you."

"Well, if tonight's any indication, I do still have some skills." Bernie squirmed to reach into her back pocket and pull out the switchblade. She tossed it onto the dirt in front of them.

"Geesh, Bernie."

"From the old days."

"What— " Paul stopped, looking around the cannery for a minute. "What happened to you? Back then, on the streets?"

"I never talk about that time. Not with anyone."

"And it's hanging there between us. I think we need to talk about it to get past it."

Bernie twirled a strand of her hair with her free hand while she thought. So much happened during those years. Some good, some bad, some horrible. She'd put it all behind her when she settled in Willow Bay. Or thought she had. But it still colored her actions, and if she wanted to move forward, to have time with Paul, it meant trusting him with her story.

Damn. This was going to be hard. She tried to pull her hand from his, but he held on tight.

"Life on the streets isn't all bad, you know. I made some friends."

"I've heard that." Paul smiled. "I'm glad you had a

gang."

"It wasn't much of a gang. Just Don, Mary, and me. We looked out for each other. Shared food and foraged goods. We rarely stole, but sometimes we had to, only taking what we needed."

She tugged hard and this time, Paul let her hand go. Picking up the blade, she turned over and over, the motion taking her back. "This was Tristan's knife."

~~~

Who the hell was Tristan? Paul leaned forward as Bernie's face went blank and she disappeared into her memories. Desperate to help, but not knowing how and not wanting her to stop, he waited. She needed to get this out.

"Tristan joined our ragtag little gang after a few months. He was older, bigger, stronger. And he seemed to care about our welfare. He and I, well… " Bernie shrugged. "You can guess that part."

Paul forced his hands to remain unclenched at the thought of someone being with his Bernie. Except, she hadn't been his Bernie back then. She'd been scrapping for her future, her very life.

"One night, Tristan said he had a job he wanted us to do. He said it would be easy money and we'd be set. We followed him even though we were uneasy. Turns out, he wanted us to hit a meth manufacturing house.

"That was way more than we wanted to take on, but Tristan wouldn't take no for an answer. He forced us to go with him."

"How?" Paul scrubbed his face. "Never mind. Not sure I want to know that."

"You don't." Bernie focused in on Paul's face. "You have to understand. We were underage. If I went to the police, reported Tristan, they'd send me back to my alcoholic parents. I wasn't going back there. Ever."

"What happened?" Paul asked.

"Tristan sent us in the front door of the supposed meth house, but no one was there. He got pissed and started checking out the house. I told Don and Mary to run, and to keep going. When you're homeless, you always carry your stuff with you, so we each had our go bags on our back."

"You didn't run with them?"

She shook her head. "I brought Tristan into our group. It was my problem to fix." She gulped, proving to Paul that this next part was going to be harder to tell.

"He saw they were gone and came at me."

Bernie raised her shirt and showed Paul the small pucker low on the side of her abdomen. "He shot you?"

"Stabbed me. With this knife." She held it up. "He thought he got me good, even left the knife in me. Turns out, he missed everything important. Still, I was bleeding and he left me there on the floor to go search the house. So I dragged myself out of the house, forced myself to stand, take a step, then another, until I couldn't see the house. I collapsed into some bushes where I could hide and regroup. I was in the process of wrapping something around me to stop the bleeding when I heard the gunshots. A whole lot of them.

I didn't wait to see how it unfolded. As soon as I heard sirens, I lit out of there. Turns out, we were within a mile of a hospital, so I got patched up."

"They didn't send you back to your parents?"

"I refused to tell them anything. One kind ER doc took pity on my and stitched up my side. I asked him if he'd heard anything about gunshots at a nearby house. He gave me a sharp look and said the only people brought to the hospital had been in body bags. Then he casually mentioned that child protective services had been called and left. I took that as my cue and slipped out."

"What about the stitches?"

"Took them out myself. I never saw Don or Mary again after that. I headed north along the coast, eventually finding my way here. Still, I live with the worry about what happened to Don and Mary and the guilt that I put them in such a dangerous situation.

"That's Tristan's fault, not yours."

Bernie tossed the knife and tapped her brain. "I know that here." Then her heart and gut. "Here and here, not so much. But I've tried to make amends."

"Hence all the rescues and helping people like Gladys."

"Yes. Though I like to think I'd do all that anyway. It feels good."

Paul stood, pulling Bernie up and into his arms. "That wasn't an easy story to tell."

"Nope."

"Thank you for trusting me with it."

"I don't trust easily. But you? I think I've found the exception."

Believe me, I will cherish this rare privilege. I guess—"—he paused to gather his thoughts—"I can understand what made you take off after Jen like that. But Bernie, God, don't ever do that to me again."

She hugged him tight. "No guarantees. I protect what's mine."

"Just as I protect what's mine," he said. "And you, my spunky, gorgeous redhead, are all mine."

"I am?" She leaned back to look up at him. The hope and trust in her eyes filled him with so much emotion, he almost couldn't stand it.

"I love you, Bernie Pedersen. I love every part of you. Even the one that scares the life out of me."

"I never thought I'd know love until you came along. You've opened my eyes to so much, Paul. I couldn't stand to lose you."

He kissed her then, gently at first, filling it with the overpowering emotion he felt for her. Promising her a future as he deepened it. She opened to him, letting him in, and he took her precious gift with abandon. It was a long time before they parted, both breathing hard.

"So we'll protect each other from now on, right?" Paul said. "No more secrets or subterfuge?"

"Agreed."

"Then let's go home and see how our girl is doing."

Hand in hand, they walked out of the cannery and home to their future.

Chapter Seventeen

Bernie and Paul walked into what looked like a party at Square Peg. Michael and Andrea were grinning widely and chatting with Jackson. Dana laughed at Juniper's antics as Jen played with her on the floor then stood when she saw them.

"There you are," Dana said.

Dirty pizza platters and half-empty sodas were spread over a couple tables.

"Who the hell is making pizza in my joint?" Bernie said.

Josh poked his head around the corner. "About time you got back. We were hungry."

"It's after midnight, and it's *my* kitchen."

"I've watched you enough to know how things work around here. And like I said, we were hungry."

"Plus, we didn't want to rehash everything again," Jackson piped in, "so we waited until you got back. Took you long enough." He eyed them as if trying to determine if they'd been fooling around.

Jen hugged Bernie, then Paul. "You guys okay now? Fight over?"

"Fight's over. We're fine." Bernie couldn't stop smiling.

"I hear the making-up part can be pretty good."

"Jen!" Both sets of would-be parents said all at once.

"I just heard, that's all," Jen said, grinning.

Bernie loved it. Jen was acting just like a teenager. Normal. "Where's Georgia?"

"Said she had some things to take care of and she'd see us tomorrow."

Bernie looked around at all the glasses of pop. "No one cracked open the beer?"

Jackson moved his hat off the chair next to him. "I'm

on duty."

"And even I don't touch your beer without permission," Josh said.

"Smart man," Bernie answered, patting his cheek. "Anyone want one?"

Josh, Paul, and Jen's dad took her up on the offer, so Bernie poured four beers, then sank down next to Paul in the chair Jackson's hat had vacated.

"Okay, now that we're all here and since the question of guardianship is a bit confused at the moment, for legalities' sake, does anyone mind if I ask Jen a few questions?" Jackson asked.

A chorus of "no" answered him.

"And Jen? Are you willing to answer some questions in front of these people?"

She nodded, threading her arm through Bernie's.

"Okay. First, here's what I know. Gavin Thompson was your mother's boyfriend. When she died, he was given custody of you because there were no relatives. At the time. Right?"

"He just wanted Mom's money."

"We're going to stick to the facts here, Jen. That's all I can work with."

"But— "

"Let him finish." Bernie pulled Jen in closer. "If you have more you want to say after his questions, you'll have a lot of people willing to listen. Okay, kid?"

"Okay."

Bernie almost laughed at the glum expression on Jen's face. Teenagers always wanted to be heard their way, and Jen seemed to be rebounding quickly from her ordeal.

"Tell us about the abduction," Jackson suggested.

"I went to the kitchen to, um, give Bernie and Paul a private moment."

Michael looked at Bernie and raised an eyebrow. Her face heated up despite her best efforts, which ticked her off to no end. Paul squeezed her knee.

"Anyhow, no sooner had I got in there when someone grabbed me from the back."

"How did he get in?" Michael asked.

"I inspected the door. No forced entry," Jackson answered. "I suspect he came in while the restaurant was open and hid until he could act."

"Makes sense," Paul said, rubbing Bernie's back.

"That's creepy, that he might have been here the whole evening," Jen said.

"What happened after that?" Jackson prodded.

"Gavin tossed me in the trunk and the car took off. I think we turned right. Seemed like we were going pretty fast, but suddenly, they hit the brakes and I was thrown against the back seat. The car made a sharp turn, so I think we headed back into town."

Bernie's ire got the better of her. "They threw you in the trunk?"

"Bernie. Let her talk," Jackson said.

"When they stopped and opened the trunk, we were in that building."

"The old cannery," Josh explained for those not from Willow Bay. "It's being torn down next week to make room for a park."

Jen looked at Paul. "You know how you found out Mom left the house and a little money to me?"

Paul nodded.

"Well, he wanted that money. Said I was going to sign everything over to him or I'd learn what pain really felt like. He said no one would listen to a runaway. They'd believe him over me."

"Never," Bernie said.

"That's what I told him." Jen grinned. "And that's when you burst in and saved me, Bernie."

"Which she will never do again on her own." Jackson leveled his best cop glare on her.

Great. Now, Bernie had two people trying to shackle her. Still, being here with Paul's hands on her, she didn't mind so much.

"Before they let me out of the trunk, I heard Gavin and the other guy talking. He said, 'Once that house sells, you'll get your money.'"

"Money?" Jackson asked.

"I don't remember anybody like that guy being around the house when I lived there. I do remember Gavin and mom having arguments about how he left all the time and came back late. And about money."

"Wow. All this drama for a couple hundred thousand dollars," Josh said. "The guy must be hard up."

"We don't know everything yet," Jackson said, grabbing his hat. "But based on Paul's digging, this Gavin person has done this before. No evidence yet that he's killed anyone."

"He killed my mother. I know he did."

"I'll include that in your statement and you can read and sign it tomorrow with everyone's blessing. Beyond that, we'll have to let the Vancouver police do their job. But I think, just based on what he's done here tonight, Gavin will be going away for a long time." Jackson stood. "I need to get to that report. Bernie, I tried to get Jen to go to the hospital. She didn't want to go."

"I'm fine."

"Did you get hit over the head?" Paul asked.

"No. Just my hands tied."

"And slapped pretty hard," Bernie said.

The bruise was already forming on Jen's cheek.

"Really, I'm fine. I just want to stay here. At home." She

hugged Bernie. Michael stiffened and Bernie looked his way, afraid he would protest. His eyes narrowed, but he gave her a slight nod.

Jackson stood. "All right, then. I trust that you," —he looked at Jen—"will be here tomorrow?"

"Yes, sir."

"Good. Stop by the station in the afternoon and we'll finalize your report."

"Yes, sir," Jen said, saluting.

Jackson frowned but said his goodbyes and left without further comment.

"I think it's time for everyone to get some sleep." Bernie turned to Michael and Andrea. "Anything else can wait until tomorrow."

"Agreed." Michael and Andrea hugged Jen goodbye and left close behind the sheriff.

"You guys really know how to add excitement to my days," Josh said. "Stop that, okay? I'd like to spend my nights with my soon-to-be-wife, not you."

Bernie punched him in the arm, then hugged him tight. Josh hugged Jen, shook hands with Paul. Dana hugged Jen and Bernie, picked Duffy up and they left for home.

"I'm beat," Jen said. "I'm going to crash."

"Where? We haven't cleaned upstairs yet."

"Oh, yeah."

"Ready to close up?" Paul asked.

Bernie checked that everything was off and put away. The dishes and mess could be dealt with tomorrow. "Ready."

"Then let's lock up and head over to my condo."

The night was clear and chilly, the stars bright in the sky as they walked the two blocks to Paul's rental. Jen and Juniper skipped ahead, the resilience of youth allowing them to slough off the night's events.

For Bernie, exhaustion was complete. She'd run the

emotional gamut tonight and, though things had ended better than she'd ever expected, she needed sleep and time to process everything.

At the condo, they set up the couch for Jen who settled in with Juniper and the TV remote.

"Good thing dogs are allowed here," Paul said.

"No way are we separating those two tonight."

"Agreed. Let's go out on the balcony," Paul suggested. Once the sliding door shut behind them, he opened his arms to her.

"Wow. What a rollercoaster," Bernie said.

"Welcome to life with kids."

"You don't have any kids, so how do you know? Umm— " She leaned back to look at his face. "Do you?"

Paul laughed. "Nope. No kids, at least, not that I know of, and I've been careful. When I bring a child into this world, I want to have the time and energy to love him or her fully. But I work with kids, so I know the chaos they can create."

"Do you want kids?"

"Sure. Eventually. Do you?"

"I've never thought of myself as mother material." She glanced inside. "But maybe."

When Paul kissed her, everything in Bernie's life clicked into place. This felt like home. He felt like home.

"We'd better stop or that kid thing might become a reality too soon."

"Don't stop."

He gaped at her.

"I don't mean we should make a kid! Geesh. And we've got a teenager in the condo. I just... " Bernie had never needed anyone before and admitting it wasn't easy. "It's not a bad idea to sleep together tonight, right?"

"What, you don't want to share a lumpy sofa sleeper

with a teenager and her dog?"

"Not really, no."

Paul smiled and kissed her again. "Then let's go to bed. I'd love to just hold you all night."

"I'd love that, too."

They admonished Jen not to stay up much longer and headed for bed. Soon, snuggled deep in the arms of the man she loved, Bernie felt a peace she'd never known come over her. Her life had started with little or no love, and now it surrounded her. First Jen, then Paul had cracked the walls she'd built up and they'd crumbled like flour just about ready to be worked into dough.

She was okay with that. Really okay.

Chapter Eighteen

Bernie woke slowly, spellbound in Paul's arms. They created a cocoon of warmth and acceptance she'd never known before. She'd lived by the mantra "never let them in," but now, every door to her heart had been smashed open. She loved Paul beyond anything she'd ever known and wanted to wake up beside him every day for the rest of her life. Did he want that?

"'Morning."

God, even his wake-up voice was sexy, all low and gruff.

"Good morning."

"You tensed up."

"You weren't supposed to notice."

"Where you are concerned, I notice everything."

She smiled and turned to him, covering her mouth. He pulled her hand away and kissed her, long and slow. "Never hide from me, my love."

"So last night wasn't just the emotion of the moment? An adrenaline love high?"

"Absolutely not. I love you, Bernie. I didn't come here looking for that, but I found it in spades. I want to be with you. Spend days and nights by your side."

"We barely know each other."

"We know enough. The rest, we'll learn as we go." He laid back, watching her, waiting.

Bernie smoothed her hand along his cheek. "I vowed never to trust people again. Since coming here to Willow Bay, I've made some real friends. I've learned the true meaning of friendship and faith. You show me at every turn that I can trust you, Paul Gibson. And I'm bursting at the seams with emotion. Yes, I love you. So much, I'm afraid to believe in it. I love how trustworthy you are. I love that you try to see all sides of the situation. I love the touch of gray showing up at your temples. The way you wear your emotions on your face. Don't ever play poker, by the way."

"Yeah, I suck at that."

"I love everything about you and that scares the hell out of me."

Paul pulled her tight to his side. "I know how hard that was for you to say. Unlike me, you don't wear your emotions on your sleeve, so I can't even describe how happy it makes me to hear the words."

He kissed her then, cementing their promise to take their relationship as far as it would go. The kiss deepened and moved into more until Bernie broke off. "We've got a teen in the next room and I need to brush my teeth."

"Then go, woman." He spanked her lightly on the bottom as she jumped out of bed. "But hurry back. Please. At least we can make out for a while."

~~~

They made it to the restaurant just in time for Michael and Andrea to pick up Jen for breakfast. Paul ran to the coffee shop—the scene of his and Bernie's ill-fated first date—and got coffees and breakfast sandwiches for them, smiling at the domesticity that tugged at his heartstrings. He'd love nothing more than to keep things just as they were right now. Him, Bernie, Jen. One family.

His phone buzzed and he glanced at the text, which burst his bubble of contentment. A lot of things still needed working out.

"Georgia just texted," he said when he got back. "She wants us all to meet after Jen's done having breakfast with Michael and Andrea."

Bernie heaved a deep sigh before she spoke. "Yeah, I guess we have to have a conversation."

An hour later, the six of them sat around the same table in the restaurant they'd been at less than twelve hours ago. Both Bernie and Jen were pots about to boil over at any moment. Before they could start sorting things out, Josh poked his head in the door.

"Can I borrow Paul for a minute?"

Paul had no idea what for, and the frown on Bernie's face said she didn't either. But he followed Josh outside closed the door behind them.

"Sure is nice to have a sunny day," Josh said.

"I hear they can be few and far between."

"They can. We had a pretty rough winter this last one. Town almost died from a lack of tourism. Normally, we make up for it in spring, summer, and fall, but we'd had a slow couple quarters before that, so it was tough. Picking up now," Josh said, nodding as he watched the cars driving by. "Yep, picking up now."

"So, I've got a meeting about to start inside," Paul said, trying to prod Josh into explaining why he'd asked to speak to him.

"Over Jen, right?"

"Yes."

"I hope that all works out."

"Me, too."

"Bernie's going to have a hard time if Jen leaves."

"She will. So will I."

"Have you got her back?"

Ah. So there it is. Paul looked at Josh for a long moment. "I love her, mayor. So yes, I've got her back."

Josh sized him up. Paul waited patiently while the man worked through the fact that Paul was going to be a serious part of Bernie's life.

"Okay," Josh finally said. "She's my friend. I had to ask."

"You're a good friend, but is that really why you came?" Paul glanced inside at the group seated around the table, chatting.

"I know you need to get back in there, but I have something for you." Josh handed over the envelope he'd been holding.

"What's this?"

"A job opportunity, if you're interested."

Paul's eyebrows lifted. He hadn't been expecting that. "From you?"

"No. County. But I'll be happy to be a reference if you decide to apply."

"Thank you. That means a lot." He waved the envelope. "I'll take a close look at this after our meeting ends." He pointed over his shoulder.

"Got it. Good luck in there."

Josh and Paul shook hands. Paul watched him get in his car and drive off, then went inside.

"I want to live here," Jen said as Paul joined the group, settling on the side of Bernie that didn't have Jen glued to it.

"I know you've found good friends here," Michael said. "We'd like to have you with us, though. I missed the first thirteen years of your life. I—we—don't want to miss any more."

"Where are we at from a legal standpoint?" Paul asked Georgia.

"I think we'll be setting precedents," she said, shaking her head. "Right now, the man who's Jen's legal guardian is in jail."

"Right where he belongs," Bernie said.

"Yes. For official reasons, we'll need to do a DNA test to prove with finality that Jen and Michael are biologically related. The county will cover that cost and I have the kits with me."

Standard Operating Procedure. Paul had done this many times.

"I have a suggestion I want you all to consider." Georgia folded her hands together on the table. "I can have Bernie and Paul designated as Jen's temporary guardians."

"Yes!" Jen said.

Georgia glared at her. "Temporary. Since things are stable here."

"How can you say that?" Andrea interjected. "She was kidnapped."

"And the man is in jail. Before and after that incident, Jen was doing pretty well here, from what I can glean."

"We all were," Bernie said.

"Then I suggest she stay here while you all get to know each other better. Michael and Andrea, you can visit Jen here. Jen, you can spend some weekends with them. I will probably suggest to the court that a three-month period be set, at which point a judge will make the final decision. The house, and any money from Jen's mother's estate, will be put in a trust until the judge resets things legally."

No one spoke. They all sat there, digesting Georgia's suggestion. Paul grinned at his former colleague. It really was the best of both worlds. It gave them all time, and time was what they needed most right now.

Michael looked at Andrea, then at Jen and Bernie, and finally, back at Georgia. "We can live with that."

"Bernie?"

"If Jen's okay with that, I'm good."

All eyes turned toward Jen. "I guess. Well, I guess that's what we have to do. After three months, will the judge listen to what I want?"

"Since we don't want you to turn into a runner once again, yes. The judge will consider many factors, including how you feel about things." Georgia stood. "All right then.

We have a plan. I'll go get those kits. Once I get everything settled legally, I'll let you all know. Bernie, you might have to answer some questions."

"I figured."

"Good. Paul, come help me?"

He got up and followed her outside, where she dug the kits out of her trunk, then pulled a box out. "Since Randy ousted you, I took a minute to gather your personal items. I brought them with me."

"Thank you." Paul took the box.

"You hadn't been happy there for a while, had you?"

Paul shook his head. "It's time for something else. Something new." He thought about the envelope in his pocket.

"Maybe you'll find something around here, close to that pizza joint, and its owner."

"I love her. Going to spend the rest of my life with her if she'll let me."

Georgia patted his arm. "You're good people, Paul. Now you'll have good people around you, too."

She headed inside to take DNA samples, but Paul sat down and opened the envelope to look at what Josh had brought him. His eyes widened as he read. This was perfect for him. An excitement he hadn't felt in quite a while welled up within him. His life was turning, changing directions, and Paul headed inside, ready to roll with it all.

Epilogue

Three months later, Bernie and Paul stood outside the restaurant on a day considered warm at the beach.

"I'm going to miss her so much," Bernie said. She would. The kid had entered their lives by chance and quickly shown her mettle, that she was a good kid despite what life had thrown at her. Now, there wouldn't be any more midnight chick flicks, or running Juniper along the beach.

"I'll miss her, too. She's wrapped herself around our hearts."

"I bet right now, she's making her bed and straightening up before she comes down here."

"She's a bit of a neat freak. Unlike you," Paul said, wrapping his arms around Bernie from behind. "I guess I'm going to have to pick up that slack, Mrs. Gibson."

Bernie looked at the simple gold band on her finger. She still couldn't get used to it. She'd gone from being a loner who needed no one to having a family, one she desperately wanted.

Paul placed his hand beside hers and their rings sparkled in the sunlight. "They look good together."

"I can't believe you talked me into such a quick wedding. Josh and Dana met months before us, and we got married before they did."

"I didn't want to wait." Paul's arms tightened around her.

"Neither did I," Bernie said, squeezing his arms. They both listened to the surf roll for a minute.

"You didn't have any problem taking off today?" Bernie asked.

"When you're a one-man show, you can set your own

schedule. At least, they've given me that leeway, and I wanted to be here for this."

"I'm glad you're here. And I'm glad you took the job."

"Me, too. I like working with kids in conjunction with the women's shelter. The town's expansion will make my job all the more necessary. These teens can be just as sullen as the kids I worked with before, but they're at risk, not already mired in some impossible situation. I've already made progress, making sure they have school supplies and clothes. I've found some of the older ones internships, or I'm getting them into jobs and training. I can already see how it's motivating some of them to finish school."

"And last night's pizza party was a huge success. I think you're right. We should do that once a month for the kids."

"If we can afford it. They about ate us out of pizza."

Bernie laughed. The party at the restaurant, alive with the chatter of about twenty teens, had been good for all of them. Jen most of all. She knew some of them.

Footfalls on the steps signaled their idyllic life was about to change. Jen bounded downstairs with the ever-present Juniper. She was decked out in thready jeans and the jacket she'd talked Paul into buying her months ago. She never went anywhere without it, no matter the weather.

Michael and Andrea followed Jen downstairs.

Jen held up her suitcase. "I'm all packed."

This was it. The moment Bernie had been dreading. Over the past three months, Jen had visited Michael and Andrea several times. She'd helped them pick out paint colors and decorations for her room, had toured the local high school. She'd even met some kids, one of which, a girl named Mary, was already moving into best friend territory. The two of them spent hours on the phone every night. Jen had made the heart-wrenching decision herself before their court date, and Bernie agreed. She'd be happy with Michael and Andrea, even if Bernie's heart was breaking a little.

As she hugged Paul, then Bernie, Jen's eyes filled with tears.

"You be good, kid," Bernie said. "Remember, your parents know best. At least, these two do."

"I'll listen. Or try to. I promise."

"We'll be down for Thanksgiving," Paul said.

"And I get to come visit next summer for a couple weeks!"

"You have my phone number," Bernie said, hugging her again. "I expect regular updates."

Jen nodded, then sobered. "I can't believe how this all turned out. And it's all because you took a chance on me, a ragged street kid."

"I saw a lot of me in you." Bernie's voice broke. "I love you, kid. Be good."

"I will." Jen's phone rang as she headed for the car. "Mary!" A pause as she listened. "Yep, heading out in a few. You'll come over tonight, right? You've *got* to see my new bedroom! And about school... "

All four adults chuckled at the nonstop monologue. Bernie could see the happiness in Michael and Andrea's faces. Her own heart might be breaking a little, but this was the right thing to do.

"Thank you, both, for making this transition work. Especially you, Bernie," Michael said. "This couldn't have been easy for you."

Another damn sheen of tears stung Bernie's eyes. She sniffed them back. "It wasn't. But it was the best thing for Jen."

"And for us. We've fallen so in love with her," Andrea said.

"She's a hard kid to hate."

"That she is. Well, we'd better get on the road. From the

sounds inside that car, plans are being made."

"Have a safe trip home to Portland," Paul said.

Bernie clutched his hand as the newly formed family drove away. "This will be a good thing for her. I know it will." Still, the sadness threatened to overwhelm her.

"She's going to thrive, thanks to you," Paul said.

"You're right." Bernie turned to wrap her arms around his neck. "I just need my heart to understand it."

"And I'll do my best to distract you." He kissed her.

God, she loved his kisses. Tightening against him, she gave herself up to her husband.

"Get a room!"

They pulled apart, laughing as Josh and Dana pulled up and got out of their car, Duffy leaping out with them. "Did we miss Jen?"

"They just left."

"Darn," Dana said, holding up a bag. "I put together a journal packet for her."

"I can mail it to her," Bernie said, taking the bag.

"That would be great. Thanks."

"You doing okay?" Josh asked Bernie.

Was she? She looked around. At her husband, her friends, her restaurant. She placed a hand over her stomach. So much had changed in her life, yanking her out of her comfort zone and into the arms of her husband. "Yes. I really am all right. Thanks to all of you."

"Good. Now, Dana and I had better get back. She locked the doors to the gift shop so we could buzz over here."

After they left, Bernie turned to Paul. "I have something to tell you."

"Does it have something to do with how protective you've become of your abdomen?"

"Ahhh, you know."

"I suspected."

"Are you happy?"

Paul wrapped her in his arms. "Happier than I ever thought I could be."

"Me, too."

"Come on. Let's go clutter up the apartment some."

Bernie laughed. "I swore you were moving things around just to mess with her."

"Jen has a good eye for details. She didn't miss a thing."

They laughed as they left the beach. Inside their apartment, they found a bouquet of flowers.

"How did they sneak these upstairs without us seeing?"

"I don't know." Paul read the card and smiled, handing it to Bernie.

Thank you. We owe you everything.

A second note, written in Jen's hand, lay next to it.

I want to be here when the baby is born.

They stared at each other.

"Did she know?"

"She couldn't have."

"She's pretty darn astute."

"One thing's for sure. We'd better make sure she's here."

"Until then, it's just you and me," Paul said.

Bernie fingered the corner of Jen's note, then turned to Paul. "Yep. Just you and me."

Exactly where she wanted to be. Home.

~~~

"You haven't called me for any assistance in a while."

Back in her own home, Gladys settled in her chair, having watched from a distance as Bernie and Paul sent their charge off to her new life. "I haven't needed any help."

"I like talking to you. You could call just to chat, you know."

"I could, but what would we chat about?"

"Life, love, maybe meeting in person one of these days."

An unusual thrill threaded its way down Gladys' back and she harrumphed to cover the sigh of contentment she'd just about uttered. "Things are fine just the way they are, Henry."

The silence between them stretched out. Gladys broke it first, wondering why. This was not her usual behavior and she needed to get things back on track.

"Did the donation for the new children's arm of the women's shelter arrive?"

"Yes, it did." All business now, Henry had tucked anything he thought about their conversation away, just as she had.

"Excellent. That will keep Paul busy and it's good for Willow Bay, too."

"You ever going to tell this town you're its matriarch and matchmaker both?"

"Never. I'd lose the ability to know what's going on. People would stop talking to me."

"One of these days, you're going to get found out, Gladys Hawthorne. And I, for one, want to be there when that happens."

"Bah! Never going to happen."

"Time will tell," Henry said, ringing off.

Yes, Gladys thought. Time will tell. Maybe Henry was right and she'd be found out eventually. But there was still so much to do, and she knew exactly where to help next.

~~~

Thank you for reading **Finding Home**, the second story in the Willow Bay series. While this series can be read in any order, the next one in the series is Chance's Are

(Dana's friend, Aimi's story.) If you enjoyed this book, please consider leaving a review wherever you prefer, and know that it would be greatly appreciated.

For new release information and news about Laurie Ryan, please join her **newsletter**.

Author's Note and Acknowledgements

During the COVID-19 pandemic, I found my happy place along the Washington Coast. Because of that, I decided I wanted to be there as much as I possibly could. What better way than to set a series there. That was the kernel that kicked off the Willow Bay series.

I made a purposeful choice not to introduce COVID-19 into this series. It's meant to lift up, to make you smile, to be a distraction, not a reminder.

Finding Home is the story that started this whole series for me. The ocean has always felt like home to me and, one day, while sitting in front of my favorite pizza place, I envisioned an older street person finding a runaway and asking the pizza parlor owner for help. Willow Bay was officially born. This story, however, seemed too focused to showcase and set up the town. Hence, Mayor Josh Morgan's story got flagship status.

No story can get to publication without a village helping to make it shine. To my wonderful critique partners, all authors I admire: Lavada Dee, Marie Tuhart, Sadira Stone, and Cari Davis. To my editor, Libby Doyle of Fairhill Editing, to my amazing cover designer, Visual Node for Graphics.

I always end with a thank you to you, my readers. I keep thinking I should put you up front on this letter because you are the reason I continue to write stories and I'm so grateful. However, always being a person who saves the best for last, you are in the spot that shows my highest regard. Thank you, thank you, thank you!

Laurie Ryan

Booklist

Contemporary romance stories by Laurie Ryan

Willow Bay Series
Last Resort
Finding Home
Chances Are (October 2021)
Tender Tide (coming in 2022)

Tropical Persuasions Series
Stolen Treasures
Pirate's Promise
Dare to Love

Standalone
Rudy's Heart
Lost and Found
Northern Lights
Healing Love
(also part of the Holiday Magic anthology)

Women's Fiction by Laurie Ryan
Show Me

Fantasy by Laurie Ryan
Survival
Enlightenment
Birthright
Awakening
Wolf's Call

Bio

Laurie Ryan writes fantasy and contemporary romance. Growing up a devoted reader, Laurie Ryan immersed herself in the diverse works of authors like Tolkien and Woodiwiss. She is passionate about every aspect of a book: beginning, middle, and end. She can't arrive to a movie five minutes late, has never been able to read the end of a book before the beginning, and is a strong believer in reading the book before seeing the movie.

Laurie lives in the beautiful Pacific Northwest, in the shadow of Mt. Rainier and a short drive to beach-walking next to the Pacific Ocean, with her handsome, he-can-fix-anything husband.

Stay in touch with the author via her newsletter or find out more at laurieryanauthor.com.

A Sneak Peek at the Third Book in the Willow Bay Series

CHANCES ARE
BY LAURIE RYAN

CHAPTER ONE

"You may now kiss the bride."

Jackson Smith clapped, then laughed along with everyone else as his friends kissed. Josh's enthusiasm about being a married man showed big time. The man had loved Dana ever since she moved here and bought one of the gift shops near the beach. His friend had been waiting for this day for a long time and had even gone along with the flower-bedecked church.

What a fool. Jackson shook his head. He had nothing against women. They were great as friends and offered a perspective that he found important. But once you let them into your life, everything changed, and nothing lasted forever. Nope, he'd never be the one waiting at the front of the church. He'd become a born-again bachelor and nothing would change that. He was happy with his life, though an occasional dalliance wasn't out of the question.

He glanced at the wedding party again, particularly at the maid of honor. He'd seen her once before, briefly, when arresting Dana's ex-husband for forging her signature. There'd been no time then to talk to her, and when he'd gone to Dana's shop the next day, she'd already left town.

Maid or matron? He couldn't see her ring finger under the bouquets she held. She intrigued him, with her long, sleek, dark hair and eyes the same color that shone with happiness while she watched her friends exit the church. Then it was her turn. She and Bernie walked down the aisle together. Josh had selected Bernadette Gibson as his best, umm, person. A non-traditional moment in an otherwise very traditional wedding.

He tried again for a glimpse of the woman's left hand. Still buried under flowers, damn it. Something about her drew him in. He'd planned on ditching the reception. Weren't they all alike, anyhow? But now, maybe he'd pop in. Just to satisfy his curiosity about the mysterious woman.

Jackson filed out with everyone else in the church, helping Gladys, Willow Bay's most familiar resident street-person. "Looking mighty fine there, Miss Gladys." He took her arm as she hobbled along.

"Thank you, Officer. For the compliment and the arm. I don't get around so well without my Mabel."

Jackson held back his head shake at the name Gladys picked for her grocery cart. She and Mabel were a staple in Willow Bay. She refused lodging help, but would always take food. The town had accepted responsibility for Gladys, and she probably ate better than most because of it. Still, she looked thinner today. And her white hair looked different.

"Did you get a new outfit?"

"Had to have a dress for the wedding." She pirouetted with surprising dexterity. "Looks pretty good, doesn't it? $3.99 at the thrift store. Even got my hair washed at Mae's."

Wondering where they'd mailed her wedding invitation, Jackson smiled at the mention of Mae's. The salon offered haircuts for free to Gladys and she loved a good deal.

"You look lovely." They'd reached her cart. "Want a lift to the reception?"

"In that thing?" She glanced at his nearby squad car. "No, thanks. Town'll think you've finally arrested me for loitering. No, Mabel and I will be just fine. It's not far, and I can keep an eye on the town. Looking forward to some good food at that reception. Oh, yes."

She and Mabel ambled their way out of the parking lot. One of Mabel's wheels wobbled, making a racket as they left. Jackson laughed. There was no one like Gladys. It hit him why she looked thinner. She usually wore two or three layers of clothing. Today, she only wore the dress, probably due to the unusually warm June day. Gladys was definitely one of a kind. He got in his squad car, intent on following the procession to the community hall until his phone beeped.

Damn.

A shoplifter at the hardware store. Who stole from a place like that? He toyed with the idea of calling and telling Mike he'd be a while, but if his wife was working the store alone at the moment, it wasn't fair to her. So instead of turning right, he turned left and was at the store in less than five minutes. He'd always loved this place. Full to overflowing with hardware and gift items, there wasn't a tourist around who hadn't browsed these aisles in search of treasures. And if you needed a part? It was well known that Willow Bay Hardware had at least one of everything.

Sure enough, Betty was on duty, though that wasn't necessarily better for the shoplifter. She stood behind the counter, her brown eyes glaring at a kid sitting on a nearby bench who didn't even look ten years old. Way too young, and in need of a good scare to set him straight, by the looks of it. Time for Jackson to put his intimidating face on. He had a special look and a low, dark tone to his voice that he used for these occasions.

"Hi, Sheriff."

"This the boy?"

"Yep. Caught him stuffing candy bars into his backpack here." She plunked the offending pack on the counter and Jackson had to hide his surprise at the bounty the kid had attempted to steal.

He came around and stood in front of the boy, whose eyes were wide open with worry. Good. He didn't have the swagger of a habitual stealer. "Stand up."

The boy did so without a second request. Another good sign.

"What's your name?"

The boy started shaking, but kept his mouth tightly closed.

"Wouldn't tell me, either," Betty said.

"So you're not talking?"

The boy shook his head, even with the fear in his face.

"All right then." Jackson turned to Betty. "He's not a local."

"I don't think so, either. I don't recognize him."

"I guess its jail until he talks." He glared at the boy. "Sit. Don't move."

He and Betty moved off to the side, both working hard to hide their grins.

"He's got decent clothes on and is clean, so probably with vacationers," Jackson said.

"That's what I thought."

"I'll take him to the station. Sooner or later, his parents will come looking for him in a panic, though I wish I didn't have to put them through that worry."

"Maybe you'll get lucky and he'll tell you his name."

"He seems more worried about the ramifications of that than of me."

"That's because the softie in you keeps oozing out, Jackson Smith."

"I am not a softie."

"Right," Betty said, chuckling. "You don't rescue cats and dogs and take them to Bernie at the pizza joint to find homes for them, right? And you don't try to rescue the stupids who park too close to the water, either."

"That's just doing my job."

"Like I said...riiiight."

"Okay, enough. I'll take him in and wait with him."

"You'll miss the mayor and Mrs. mayor's wedding reception."

The woman with a sparkle in her dark eyes flashed through Jackson's mind, and he found himself wishing there were another way. "You missed the wedding."

"I'm closing up after you and the boy leave and joining Mike there."

"Go enjoy. I'm fine. A momentary regret touched him. He'd never find out if the woman was married or single. Probably better that way.

They both put their stern faces back on and soon the kid was ensconced behind the screen in the squad car's back seat.

"Last chance, kid. Ready to give me your name and tell me where you're staying?"

The boy looked so little in the back seat. And miserable, as he shook his head once again.

"So be it." Jackson closed the door and headed back to his two-cell station, hoping it wouldn't be long before the parents realized their son was missing.

Because as much as he tried to deny it, he really did want another glimpse of the dark-haired beauty from the wedding.

~~~

Aimi Larson toyed with the edge of her champagne glass, trying to decide what had tossed her into this melancholy. Her best friend, now happily married, snuggled on the dance floor with her husband, swaying to the notes of some love song. Cheek to cheek. Heart to heart.

What did that feel like, that kind of love? She could see it in their eyes, in how they touched often. How they could be across the room and still aware of each other, to have that smile meant only for them, like they had a secret no one else was privy to.

Aimi had wanted that, had believed in it right up until she'd reached her testosterone limit. She'd started her career and her relationships wanting strength around her. Cured of that wish, she'd sworn off men period. No one would ever make choices for her again or keep her from getting what she wanted. So she was here solo and she'd given up on love, at least for herself. Aimi was happy for her friends, but this kind of love wasn't for her. She did better on her own and she liked living alone. Being free to work long hours because she wanted to, not because some status symbol was being dangled in front of her, then the offer withdrawn after the work was done. Free to make her own choices, not be bulldozed by some guy who thinks he knows what she needs better than she does.

Free to sleep with someone or say no. The guy at the wedding had driven that realization home. Yikes. Tall, more muscular than she normally went for, but on him, it totally worked. Short, dark hair that still showed a tight natural curl. And those eyes. Amber, like a tiger's. When he glanced her way, they had seared her soul. He looked familiar. Had she seen him before?

She'd decided right then and there, standing in front of the church with her friends, that she would approach him at the reception. No strings, just a night of harmless flirting. She'd be heading back to Spokane tomorrow anyhow.

Then he'd disappeared. She'd seen him walk out of the church, then nothing. Damn it.

"Hey, why the glum face?" Dana said, sitting down beside Aimi. Her friend's curls had started to undo themselves. Dana was cursed with hair almost as straight as hers. They both fought to get curls to stay.

"Come on," Dana said. "You're supposed to be happy. Having fun."

She was right. This wasn't a moment for introspection. Her best friend had just gotten married. Aimi smiled. "I am happy. For you."

"You'll find someone one of these days, you know."

Aimi shook her head. "Not part of my agenda."

"I know you've sworn off men, but there is someone out there who's the perfect yin to your yang. I feel very certain of that."

"Not for me. And I'm all right with that." Aimi buried the hint of regret. "Come on. Let's dance." She stood and grabbed Dana by the hand, heading for the dance floor.

~~~

More information can be found at Amazon, Barnes & Noble, Kobo, or Apple Books. As well, you can find out more about Laurie Ryan and her books on her website: www.laurieryanauthor.com

THANK YOU FOR READING MY BOOK.
Laurie Ryan